THE MOUNTAINS OF YELLOWSTONE

A NOVEL

BY

WILL STEVENSON

CHAPTER ONE

Prologue

In the northwest corner of Wyoming is a majestic expanse of primitive landscapes which is Yellowstone National Park. The land is alive with the brutal harshness of ancient struggles between animals and the environment and between predators and prey. In this mix of mountains, meadows, plateaus and forests, the primal struggle for survival plays out season after season.

This struggle is staged within the backdrop of the dramatic geodynamic environment found all over the Yellowstone area. Water and heat combine to produce a primordial mix of fragile yet lethal features. The land wears the scars from the fires that are all too frequent in the park. Ranging throughout these mountains and plateaus are the valleys where, during the summer months, most of the animals reside.

A land of mountains, Yellowstone's average elevation is over seven thousand feet with many peaks reaching ten thousand feet. The largest high altitude lake in North America, Lake Yellowstone, is surrounded by four mountain ranges that reside within the borders of the Park. The Red and Washburn Ranges are found completely within the bounds of the park. The Adsaroka and Galitan ranges only lend a portion of their peaks to Yellowstone.

Within the recesses of these peaks is where most of the tourists can be found. Within the Mountains of Yellowstone, this place where man once dwelt, he is now only a casual visitor.

CHAPTER TWO
Old Buffalo

He stood six foot five inches at the withers and weighed in just under two thousand pounds. His head was huge and hung from his broad shoulders like it was stuck to the side of a wall. His mane was thin and shaggy. The hair on top of his head was darker than his facial hair to the point that it looked as if he was wearing a wig. Hanging off his chin and running along the bottom of his neck, the mane resembled the beard of an old mountain man. There was a blending where the hair around his head merged into his shoulders. It appeared as if he was wearing a fur coat over his shoulder that ended at his waist. His eyes were set on the side of his head and just above his dark eyes and back on his head, his horns jutted out and turned towards the sky. They were thick and round, tapering to a sharp point. He was old and had lived through many harsh winters in the park. He had survived many seasons of fighting for a mate on the floor of Hayden Valley. Those days were over now. He was losing his strength and his will to mate. He bore the rugged scars of the past battles with young bulls to maintain his dominance and his right to breed. Now he stayed away and kept to himself. The days in front of him were fewer than the days in the past and this would most likely be his last season.

He was lame from his last encounter with a wolf pack. He had lived. At first he ran, but they could easily follow. The wolves cornered him and he had no choice but to stand his ground. That is what saved him that day, he stood his ground. He was on a high point in the bend of a river. A sharp drop off on three sides meant that the wolves could not get behind him. All they could do was a frontal attack. He was too old and too tired to run. If he had run, the exertion would have worn him down until he could not have fought back. They would have won and his life would have been over. But he had been cornered. He still had the strength to fight and the wolves did not want to face the horns of a bull bison. The wolves knew that an injury could mean the end of their own life. One of the young wolves risked a frontal attack. A turn of head caught the wolf with a horn under a front leg. He pulled up and back, impaling the wolf in the chest. A toss of his head and the wolf went flying into the air and landed fifteen feet away in the river. His side torn open by the point of the horn. The wolf struggled to make it to shore but the current carried it downstream. The rest of the wolf pack sat and waited. Waiting for darkness. Maybe darkness would give them an advantage and they could bring down this once mighty beast. Twilight came and the full moon rose high in the sky. There would be no darkness tonight. The wolves moved on and the old buffalo lived to die another day.

CHAPTER THREE

Stephanie Beginning

The Tennessee River cuts through the foothills of the
Appalachian Mountains in the southeast corner of Tennessee.
Alternating ridges, valleys and mountains define the landscape.
Atop one of these mountains is a small community where
Stephanie had spent her life. She was just two years old when her
family purchased a three bedroom house on a corner lot just a
short walk from the small commercial district of Signal Mountain,
a bedroom community of Chattanooga. Back before the Civil
War, there was an outbreak of disease in Chattanooga. Some of
the wealthy families believed that the bad air in the city was the
cause of the illness. They established a small community on the
top of Signal Mountain. Homes were built along the ridge line
providing grand vistas of the City, the Tennessee River and
surrounding countryside.

Stephanie pulled out of her driveway and headed for the
interstate . She was in a Ford F350 Super Duty pulling a twenty-
nine foot fifth wheel trailer. It was nineteen hundred miles to
Yellowstone and Stephanie planned to make the trip in seven
days. She had a job waiting, working in a campground for the
summer season in Yellowstone National Park and she had to be
there by the first of May. She was doing it for the experience and
the ability to live for six months in one of the most beautiful and
majestic places in the world. It had taken years to get to the point

where she could make the trip. She had always wanted to travel and explore but was tied down by her career and family. The time had finally come and she was on her way. Her husband was supposed to make the trip with her, but at the last minute he backed out. His excuse was that he wanted to work a few more months to buy himself a new toy, a high performance Mustang.

This was a return trip for Stephanie, she had vacationed in Yellowstone with her husband and son years before. It was a wondrous place and she was looking forward to spending the season there. Stephanie was burnt out, feeling hopeless and had come to the end of her rope. She was trying to jump start her life. She decided to make a change and see if things improved, see if she could shake the depression and hopelessness she felt. Stephanie had wrestled with these feelings for years, not knowing with any certainty why she was unhappy. She had not found happiness in her marriage and had drifted apart from her husband. He just wanted to go to work and sit at home watching TV. Her son was a joy that turned into heartbreak when she had trouble letting go after he grew up and went to college. And then there was her practice. She was a veterinarian and the burdens of running her business had gotten to the point were they were overwhelming.

The tipping point for Stephanie came out of left field. She came to her decision to take action after attending a continuing education program at the local Veterinary Association. The speaker presented a program that spoke to Stephanie. The speaker's program was about compassion fatigue within the Veterinary practice. She had been a Veterinarian for twenty eight years and had never heard the term. She listened with interest as the speaker described the condition. It was a malady that afflicted individuals that work with the victims of trauma such as nurses, first responders, therapist and yes animal welfare workers. People who suffered from Compassion Fatigue exhibited symptoms of hopelessness, constant stress and anxiety, a decrease in the ability to experience pleasure and a persistent, pervasive negative outlook on life. As she listened to the speaker, she felt as if he was talking about her.

Stephanie was confused about her feelings and had struggled long and hard trying to determine why she felt the way she felt. She had never considered the possibility that pet euthanasias had anything to do with her feelings. This was just one more thing to think about, another item in the list to ponder. It had been Stephanie's tipping point. She knew in her heart that she could not wait any longer, she had to change course, find a new life. She wanted to be happy.

The truck roared to life as it accelerated up the on ramp onto interstate 24 and headed west. After a short dip down into Georgia the interstate turned north, crossing the Tennessee River. She motored up Monteagle without any difficulty and turned left when she reached Murfreesboro. Stephanie wanted to see the country side and planned to bypass as many big cities as she could on this trip. She did not have a lot of experience driving the truck while pulling the trailer and did not want to get tangled up in any big city rush hour traffic.

CHAPTER FOUR

Old memories

Stephanie had a lot of time to think as the miles rolled by on her
way west. She listened to the radio as she drove and put on a
channel with the songs that she grew up with. A song can tie a
person to a place or event and becomes part of the sound track of
their life. She was remembering her childhood and the friends
and adventures she had.

Stephanie wanted a different life and struggled to understand
her feelings. For years she had felt that there was something
missing. She was proud of the accomplishments, but there had to
be more. As the miles rolled by, she did a mental inventory,
examining each time period and relationship in her life. A song
would come on the radio and it would key her to a time, a place or
an event.

Somewhere near Kansas City an Elvis Presley song came on the
radio that she remembered. It was called "Old Shep" and it was
about a young boy and his dog. The song took Stephanie back to
when she was six or seven years old and in love with the
neighbor's dog. She had always wanted a dog of her own but her
parents would not allow it. The dog next door was the next best
thing. Back in those days, people let their dogs out in the morning
and the animal was free to run around all day long. Stephanie
and the neighbor's dog went everywhere together. Signal
Mountain was a small community that had less than ten thousand

souls in residence. Stephanie and her four legged friend would roam the fields and woods that surrounded the town, exploring every nook and cranny. They were inseparable.

One summer, the neighbor's dog got pregnant and had puppies. Stephanie was excited and hopeful that her father would relent and she could have a dog of her own. Every morning she was up out of bed before anyone else and over to the neighbor's back yard checking on the puppies. Her mother would call her back to eat breakfast and she would scarf down her food and return to the puppies.

One morning she woke up early to the plaintiff wail of the dog next door. She dressed and hurried out the door, over to the the neighbor's back yard to see what was wrong. Her neighbor was in the backyard standing next to a bucket and shooing his dog away. As she walked up to him, he turned raising his hand telling her not to come over. It was too late, she could see the puppies in the bucket covered in water. He had drown the puppies. Stephanie stood in horror as she looked at the lifeless bodies floating in the water. She rushed forward, towards the bucket, but the neighbor stepped in front of her blocking her path. He told her to go home but Stephanie could not move, could not even think, she was devastated and inconsolable. The neighbor reached out to turn her back towards her house. Stephanie railed at the prospect of his touch, turned and ran to her house. She found her mother in the kitchen and threw herself into her embrace, crying in her arms.

As she listened to "Old Shep" tears started flowing down her checks. The memory was as vivid as if it had happened yesterday. She pulled over on the side of the road and cried uncontrollably for what seemed like forever. Even now, she could not understand how anyone could drown puppies. The memories of that day had laid buried for years. In hindsight, as she drove through the corn fields of Kansas, she came to realize that this event had been the motivation for her becoming a Veterinarian. She wanted to help animals, protect them and take care of them.

11

CHAPTER FIVE

Jason leaving

Jason left from Las Vegas for the drive up to Yellowstone. The route took him through Nevada, Arizona, Utah and Idaho. The landscape was barren and seemed devoid of life. Jason could recognize the grandeur of the desert vistas and rock formations that populated the far reaches of his vision. The Virgin River Gorge is a wonder of the West. All Jason could see was the walls of stone rising up to surround him in a gray monotone that was only punctuated by the shadows of the odd cloud that drifted above.

The contract of employment had a start date of May 1st and it was late April. Jason had five days to drive the seven hundred and fifty miles to the Park's west entrance.

Long before ever ending up in Las Vegas, Jason had wanted to go explore Yellowstone. Jason had hopes and dreams like everyone else, but as the years went by, some of these dreams fell away. One dream that Jason clung to was his desire for a life of discovery and adventure, and travel was going to be his vehicle to this life style. Jason wanted to see the United States and all the majestic places that it held. He had deferred this dream for many years until he came to a point where he knew that if he did not go now, he would never go. For one thing he started having problems with his health. Living in Las Vegas had given him a view of a possible future that scared him and he realized that there was no time like the present to get started. What was he waiting for anyway? Anyone could see that by this time in his life, Jason was way worn and weary. He was certain that if he stayed in Las Vegas, he would end up as one of the countless faces, disconnected and alone, staring into a slot machine's display, wasting his life and money while waiting to die. He was stuck in Las Vegas, but he was going to change that. Jason was going to become the author of his own life.

Jason had explored or traveled through most of the United States. One part of the country that he always seemed to miss was the area around Wyoming and Montana and right in the middle of this area was Yellowstone. He was going to Yellowstone! His plan was to Walmart hop up the highway. These stores are everywhere and for business reasons, they allow people traveling through to park their motor homes overnight in their parking lots. It makes good business sense for Walmart, the parking lots are empty in the evening hours and the RVers shop at the store. The travelers like Walmart, it's free to park there and they have security that patrols the lots. Before leaving, Jason had planned out his trip so that he would just travel a few hundred miles a day.

Jason could not just go and stay in the park for an extended period of time. The cost of staying in an RV park for that period of time made that impossible, so Jason needed another way. If he had a job in or around the park, he could stay and really experience all that the park had to offer. Working in the park would let him stay five months and would give him the opportunity to explore on his off time.

The place that he wanted to work for was an RV park in the geographical middle of Yellowstone. The RV park required about twenty two other adventurers to work there. Jason applied and was offered a job which required him to commit to about thirty five hours per week with two days off. This was the perfect arrangement allowing him to explore on his off time and to have something to do when he was not hiking. He could not spend all of this time exploring. He also needed a little social interaction and he hoped he would find a few like-minded adventurers among his fellow employees.

Jason's home while he stayed in Yellowstone would be an old bus. It had started its life in the service of Greyhound Bus Company in nineteen sixty carrying people between cities on the highway. Greyhound would operate new buses for about ten years before they were sold to other operators. Eventually it was retired from passenger service and was purchased sometime in the late nineteen seventies by a private party. This is when the vehicle was converted to a motor home.

To Jason, there was just something about the way an old bus looks. It was thirty five feet overall in length and eight feet wide. Some of the windows along the side had been removed and replaced with panels which made her look more like a motor home than a commercial bus. The edges of the bus were rounded and smooth letting the wind slip past as she motored on towards the next town. She was adorned with lights that framed the structure in the night, making an outline or silhouette of the bus. It was the lines that gave her a classic look and turned the heads of the passengers in the lesser vehicles that shared the road. She was built for the open road and that fact wasn't open for debate. She had been designed for traveling between cities, safely carrying forty seven passengers and the driver to their destination. She was unique, not the same RV that everybody else had and for Jason, it could not have been any other way. She too was way worn and weary. The paint was scratched and pealing in spots and there was the occasional dent here and there. She had everything that any RV would have including, a living room, a kitchen, a bathroom, and a bedroom. She was cooled by an air conditioner on the roof and heated by a propane furnace. She had a water heater to bathe and wash dishes. A generator provided power when it was needed and the bus was not connected to shore power. The refrigerator ran on both electricity and propane and the kitchen included a stove with an oven and a microwave.

14

The interior showed her age. Wood paneling was the style when she was converted to a motor home. The ceiling had a fabric lining and there was shag carpet throughout the rooms. She may have been dated but she had all the comforts of home.

As Jason drove north on Interstate 15 he imagined his future and fought against the memories of the past. He tried not to travel back to his youth, but the endless miles and wide open spaces left him at the mercy of his memories. It had been a long journey to arrive at this place and time and water had rushed under that bridge at an unimaginable rate. Playing back on his life, Jason could not believe how quickly the time had gone. Life is what happens around the fringes of every day routine. You get up every day and go to work or about your routines and mixed in and around the edge is your life. He had been living in Las Vegas and just treading water. He had spent the past thirty years in a job that he did not like. Jason had to make a living like everyone else and although the best things in life may be free, the necessities cost money. He was divorced and had been alone for a number of years. Fifty percent of American first marriages end in divorce. Sixty seven percent of second marriages end in divorce. He was a two time loser.

Jason had resigned himself to the realization that he was not relationship material. He had a lifetime of trying and failing. He believed that he could not go through it again. The transformation that is required to be in a loving caring relationship. Allowing another person to know the secrets only a lover shares and to merge his being with another and know that only she fills the voids in his soul, making him feel whole, complete. It was not the falling in love, but the hell that he went through when it ended. And for Jason, it had always ended. Sometimes it was his decision, sometimes not, who decided did not matter. Jason believed that the accumulation of heartache and disappointment had come to a critical mass, one more straw and he would be irreversibly broken.

CHAPTER SIX

Stephanie arrives

Stephanie arrived in Yellowstone late in the day and drove to the Mammoth Hot Springs area to the only open campground. She was not familiar with how to hook the trailer up to the services provide at the campground. She had always relied on her son or husband to connect the camper to the facilities. She walked around the trailer, staring at the electrical connections and appearing helpless for a few minutes. A neighbor saw her struggling to hook up and came out to help her get things set up.

Stephanie was a few days early. She had planned a few extra days for the trip up just in case something went wrong. She spent these extra days reading and hiking around the campground. She explored the nearby town of Gardiner, passing shops and restaurants that all had signs promising to open in the next week or two. Her arrival date came and she moved down to the Fishing Bridge Campground and with the help of a fellow camper, she was able to back her rig into its assigned space.

Training began the next day and it was an all day affair. Six hours of training per day for two weeks in a windowless room. She was a guest service agent and needed to learn the reservations system. The program was antiquated, it did not have a graphical user interface. It used "F" keys. Stephanie was not very computer savvy, and in the past everything was usually done for her by her employees. She was okay with clicking icons on a computer screen, but what were these "F" keys that the program used? Before she came to Yellowstone, she didn't really know what an "F" key was.

Stephanie settled in to a routine of training in the morning and short hikes in the late afternoon. She was rethinking her decision to come to Yellowstone on her own. She was living alone for the first time in twenty eight years. She had met a number of her coworkers, who were mostly couples. They kept to themselves after the training was done for the day and this left Stephanie on her own. In her life in Signal Mountain she was seldom alone. She knew everyone on the mountain and everyone knew her. She looked forward to the day the park opened and the visitors began to arrive.

CHAPTER SEVEN
Driving In

Jason's trip up Interstate 15 was uneventful and he finally made it to the west gate of Yellowstone. Jason pulled into the park and began a slow trip to the park's center and his new campground home. Winter still had a firm grip on Yellowstone. The roads had been plowed regularly and the asphalt warmed up enough in the daylight to melt off all the snow and ice. Alongside the road were walls of ice left as the plows had cut their way through. These walls sometimes exceeded five or six feet in height. It was reminiscent of what it must be like to ride a luge sled down a track with ice walls on either side.

The road into the park from the west entrance followed a river up a small valley. The valley alternated between meadows and stands of pines as it slowly climbed upward. The river banks broke the blanket of white as it zig and zagged back and forth on the valley floor.

A few miles into the park, the bus rounded a bend and came up behind three buffalo walking in the road. This was the first time Jason had seen an actual buffalo in the wild. They were headed in the same direction as the bus and they were taking their sweet time getting there. The buffalo lumbered as they walked. Picking up their front legs like it was deliberate each and every time they did it. Jason was excited to see the buffalo but that lasted only as long as it took for him to realize that they were not going to yield the road. He was following buffalo down the road at three miles an hour. Thinking about it, Jason couldn't fault them. Anyone would have walked on the road under those conditions. As far as the eye could see, the park was covered with snow and it was many feet deep. Winter was ending and the buffalo had spent most of their energy reserves. The easiest way around was to walk down the plowed roads.

Jason's first hurdle in Yellowstone was to figure out how to pass the buffalo. He had read all of the pre-employment material that had been sent to him and nowhere in that material was there a protocol for passing buffalo. He had to wing it. The road came to a long straight uphill grade and if he was going to get passed the buffalo, this was the time and place. The bus was in low gear going slow and he pulled into the opposite lane. The buffalo split up, two on his left and one on his right. They left a hole in the middle and he made his passing attempt. He didn't want to scare them so, he went slowly. Barely faster than they were walking. As he pulled alongside the ones on the left, he was eye to eye for a moment. A buffalo's huge dark eyes are on the side of its head. The beast was watching him as the bus passed. The bus managed to make it passed without any bumps or bruises.

The American Buffalo found refuge in Yellowstone. Most people are familiar with the song that has the verse" Oh give me a home, where the buffalo roam." The buffalo or bison once roamed as far east as the Atlantic seaboard. They were found in the far reaches of the Great Northwest of Canada and down into the State of Durango in Mexico. They are an impressive animal that can reach twelve feet in length and stand six feet tall at the withers. A male can weigh in at two thousand pounds. They are capable of jumping over a six foot obstacle and can run at speeds of up to forty miles an hour.

Buffalo are best remembered as residents of the great plains of America. From the earliest occupation of America, these animals were the key to survival for the Native Americans. On the American prairie, they were more numerous than the stars in the night sky. The tribes relied on them for food and shelter and used every part of the carcass, wasting nothing.

It was only when the European Settlers began to migrate west that the buffalo's days became numbered. In the 1880's there was a great slaughter. Some believed that killing the buffalo was the path to defeating and civilizing the Plains Indians. They were exploited for their pelts with millions of animals killed, skinned and left to rot where they laid. Trains crossing the prairie would stop to allow passengers to shoot and kill buffalo from their train cars.

The population was reduced to a total of five hundred and forty one animals. Ranchers are credited with saving them from extinction. Buffalo populations exist on private ranches and today their numbers total about five hundred thousand. On public lands there are about thirty thousand with only about half that number allowed to roam free. Yellowstone is the only place where buffalo have lived continuously since prehistoric times.

It was early in the year and parts of the park had not opened. Jason's destination was behind locked gates. He had been given the combination to the lock that allowed him access. He opened the gate and continued on until he reached the Fishing Bridge RV campground. Jason had been given a space number for the spot where he was supposed to park his bus. Fishing Bridge was located at about eight thousand feet and the snow was at least six feet deep. All of the roadside signs were completely covered. It went slowly, but Jason was able to find the RV Park and pulled into the parking area. He got out and looked for someone to give him directions to his site and discovered that the place was deserted. Jason walked into the camping area and looked until he found the place where he was supposed to park. In order to get into his assigned space, he would have to go around a loop and then backup his bus into the spot.

The campground had been plowed and a path was created allowing a single vehicle to navigate the loop. The walls of snow that shouldered all the roads were present and all around the RV park. Jason started down the loop and when he came to the turn around, he discovered that the plow had not made enough space for him to make the turn. He had to back up and inch his way around the loop. Finally the bus was in front of its space. It too had been plowed and there was just enough room for the bus to back in with about a foot to spare on each side. The bus squeezed into the space and Jason plugged in the electrical service. Finally, he had made it. At last, there he was, parked in Yellowstone, ready for his next adventure as a cashier. The bus was parked in a freezer with a six foot wall of snow and ice completely surrounding the bus.

When he left Las Vegas, it was in the eighties. Here it could not have been more than forty five degrees. Yellowstone was going to put the bus's heater to the test.

The Fishing Bridge area is located on the northwest side of Lake Yellowstone. The government has determined this area is prime grizzly bear habitat. Fishing Bridge is located at one end of Pelican Valley. This valley has sides that faced south and is at an altitude where bears like to make their dens. Being south facing, the sun hit the side of the valley earlier in the year. This is something the bears like. Pelican Valley slopes down and feeds into the Fishing Bridge area. This resulted in a lot of human-bear contact.

The RV park was cut out of the side of a gently sloping hill. The main entrance road continued up the hill while loops branched off the main road as it climbed in elevation. At its farthest point, the main access road reached more than a half mile up the side of the hill. In total, there were three hundred and forty parking spots for RV's. These were parking spots not RV spaces. They really could not be called camp sites. The parking spaces were so close together, that it was hard to do anything outside of the RV. Picnic tables and fire rings were not provided and open fires were not allowed.

21

The Mountains of Yellowstone

22

CHAPTER EIGHT

Summer Job

The Campgrounds, hotels, stores and other facilities in Yellowstone are part of the National Park, but not run exclusively by the Park Service. The government contracts with private industry to provide the services that the park guests require. These concessionaires run the hotels, campgrounds and the tours. They pay a part of the proceeds to the government and keep the rest for their efforts. The employees of these private companies are paid minimum wage for their time. To most of the seasonal employees, the real compensation for working in Yellowstone is the opportunity to explore and experience the park. The term of the contract for working at the campground was for five and a half months and required thirty five hours of work a week. This left time to hike and explore this amazing corner of the universe.

Twenty two employees were required to fully staff and properly run the campground. Most were older retired couples and were there on a similar mission. They wanted to experience the park and this was their way of staying busy and staying in Yellowstone. Almost all of the other employees had an RV of some sort or another. The other employee's rigs ranged from expensive class A RVs to inexpensive pull behind trailers. All the employees stayed in the same section of the RV Park. It was a small little community mixed in with the general public.

A number of the campground's employees were returning from

working in previous seasons. Some had been to the park five or six years in a row. Every summer they returned to Yellowstone for the summer season. The campground had five categories of jobs. The highest category were the administrative positions which included the general manager and the office manager. Guest service agents, cashiers and attendants filled out the list. The attendants were basically in charge of maintenance and cleaning.

CHAPTER NINE

Stephaine's Training

Stephanie had signed up to work as a reservation agent. This position required two weeks of training to learn the computer program. The training lasted from nine in the morning till four in the afternoon. It was a little daunting for Stephanie, she had relied on her staff to handle all the computer stuff at her practice. She had always been the person with all the superior skill and knowledge and everyone had been there to support her. Now she was just a worker bee along with everyone else.

Stephanie was bright, but had also relied on determination to get her through vet school. It took her a little longer to pick up the material than she believed it should have. There was a young couple in the training that seemed to fly through the material. Stephanie began to worry about her decision to come to Yellowstone.

The group broke for lunch everyday and would walk to a nearby cafeteria to eat. Everyone would sit around a table and talk. Mostly it was about the training and everything that they needed to learn. Slowly, Stephanie began to get to know the other employees. After training everyone headed home and disappeared into their respective RVs. It was still very cold outside and all the trails were still closed. Staying warm was the priority.

Cell phone service was not available in Yellowstone and access to the Internet was only available at a nearby hotel. Stephanie was cut off from the outside world and this left Stephanie alone with no other option but to think about her life. She found a shelf of books in the main office of the RV park and picked one to read in defense of the voices that constantly debated in her head. She found herself sleeping more than she had ever done in her life. In the morning she would lay half asleep for hours, thinking about her son, her marriage or her business. Only when the time to leave for training approached would she rise and dress to leave.

CHAPTER TEN

Jason Settles In

Jason settled into his spot in the park and decided to check to see if anyone had showed up. It was a short walk to the main office building. which was being opened up as Jason was approaching. Plywood was covering all the large glass windows. He wondered if that was to keep the winter out or to prevent someone from breaking in. A bobcat was clearing snow from around the trash receptacles and another crew was taking plastic wrapping off all of the signs around the main office and in the parking lot.

The front door was locked. Jason circled the building searching for an entrance. At the rear center of the building a doors said "Employees Only" and he gave it a tug. It opened. Inside he found employees in small groups working around various projects in the building. Everyone ignored Jason as he gave himself a tour. Finally, he asked someone where he could find the campground manager. He was directed down the hall to an office in the back corner of the building. He found two rooms, one was a break room and the other was an office. The office was empty. He checked out the break room. A number of tables were in use with individuals and small groups sitting and talking.

Someone looked up and acknowledged his presence and Jason introduced himself and asked if the general manager was around.

The manager was away at another location where training was being provided to the registration agents. She would return in several hours and he could find her in the office next door at that time.

Jason made himself some tea, sat down and began listening to the conversations that were taking place in the room. Everyone there was in the maintenance department and were not regularly stationed at the campground. He sat for awhile getting a feel for the kind of employees that he would be meeting. Everyone was retired or semi-retired and had come to Yellowstone to keep active and make a little money to supplement their retirement.

A half hour or so later, Jason returned to the bus and waited there for the general manager to return. He sat down to rest and before he knew it, he was fast asleep. He had been living at about two thousand feet in elevation while in Las Vegas. The Fishing Bridge area is at about eight thousand feet. The change in elevation meant that he was going to experience a lack of energy until he got acclimated. Jason slept right through the next two hours and when he woke, it was too late to meet anyone. He was fussing around the bus when there was a knock on the door. At the door, a diminutive lady in her late sixties introduced herself as Pam, the general manager. In her hands was a home baked loaf of bread and a gift to welcome Jason to the campground. They exchanged a few words about what was going to happen the next day and Jason thanked Pam for her housewarming present. He excused himself with a promise to come see her in the morning.

CHAPTER ELEVEN

Yellowstone Veterans

Jason awoke at first light. He rolled over, hugging the two extra blankets he had used to stay warm in his ice box. Warm and toasty, all wrapped up in blankets, he did not want to climb out of his cocoon. Jason's mind was too full of what the day might bring to return to sleep so finally he got up and knocked around the motor home for a couple of hours. The meeting with Pam was at about eleven o'clock.   The sun climbed a little higher in the sky and he went out to check the status of the bus. The bus was parked in a freezer and he was concerned that the electrical connections or the water hose might have some difficulty in the environment. He walked between the side of the bus and the six foot wall of ice. The jacket he wore was not enough. As he checked the connections, he noticed a neighbor directly to the rear, who was doing the same. The neighbor gave him a friendly hello and he walked over to shake his hand. The neighbor said his name was Mike and that he and his wife Hazel were there to work through the summer season. Jason introduced himself and explained that he too was there to work.

"I'm here to be a guest service agent." Mike began. The wife is a guest service agent too."

Jason explained "I have been hired as a cashier."

"Are you up here by yourself?" Mike asked.

"It's just me." Jason responded.

Jason finished checking the connections on the bus. Everything looked like it made it through the night okay. He was standing behind the bus while Mike was checking his rig. He finished and they leaned up against the back of Mike's pickup truck and talked for a while.

Mike invited Jason inside his trailer where he met Hazel. When they entered the trailer, Hazel was standing at the stove cooking eggs and pancakes. Mike offered an invitation to breakfast and Jason eagerly accepted.

The conversation during breakfast was a basic introduction to who was who and when and how they ended up in Yellowstone.

"Where are you from?" Hazel asked.

"Las Vegas." Jason replied. Jason explained his circuitous route to Yellowstone which included an extended stay in Las Vegas.

Mike gave a little of the history of how he and Hazel had found their way to Fishing Bridge.

"I am a retired police officer." Mike began. "I spent my entire working life on the Idaho State Police Force. Our home is in a small town in the southern part of Idaho. As a State Police officer, I was required to work all over the state."

As Mike talked Jason looked around the inside of the trailer. Hazel had done an excellent job of creating a homey atmosphere. Family pictures hung on the wall with mementos and knickknacks from their travels. Among the pictures was a photograph of Mike and Hazel when they were just married forty years ago.

Mike had put on weight throughout the years and he was rounded in the way a man gets when he has come to the point where suspenders are required to keep his pants from falling down. He had lost most of his hair, wore bifocals and steel toed boots. It would be hard to guess that Mike had been a police officer. He was mild in his manner, polite and patient. He was quick to smile and always genuinely interested in how other people were doing.

"What did you do in the real world Hazel?" Jason asked.

"In my life prior to retiring, I had been a high school English teacher." Hazel replied. She too had put on a few pounds over the years. Anyone could tell that Hazel was smart. She had grown up in a time where there had been little outside of the home available for smart women. She had met Mike during college and it would be a safe bet that she helped Mike get through the tough courses. Hazel had spent her life teaching rules but was not necessarily a compulsive rule follower. She had a way of assessing a person, and figuring out where they were in their understanding of a topic. Hazel had the patience to allow a person to come to their own understanding through their own process. She had been a good teacher, but she had not been challenged by her job.

Mike and Hazel had raised their family and now they were eager for the promise of their golden years. For their entire lives they had lived in small town America. Their town in Idaho had about forty thousand in residence and they knew everyone and everyone knew them. It had been their dream to purchase a travel trailer and journey around the country.

"So it was a short drive for you to get here." Jason asked.

'No." Mike said with a smile. "We took a little trip before we came here. Hazel turned her attention from the eggs on the stove and smiled at Mike when he said this. Mike continued. "When we left five months ago, we headed for the west coast and began a great circle, following the coast south. At the Mexican border we turned left and toured southern Arizona and New Mexico. Then it was on to Texas and the gulf coast. Another left turn at Florida and it was up the east coast. Finally in New England we turned left again and crossed America until we reached Yellowstone. We plan to work through the season."

This is where they were going to finish their trip. They were going to work in Yellowstone Park for the summer season. This was not their first trip to Yellowstone. Living in Idaho,

Yellowstone was in their back yard and through the years they had visited Yellowstone on numerous camping trips. They had always loved the place and had promised themselves that after they retired they would work in the park for the summer season. With this grand tour around America and the long stay at Yellowstone, they were launching the next chapter in their lives.

It was easy to see that Mike and Hazel were truly and deeply in love. They complement each other in a way that only two people who had shared a lifetime could.

Finally it came time for Jason to start heading towards his 11 o'clock appointment. Jason mused on the morning and the breakfast they had shared. He looked forward to the opportunity to get to know both Mike and Hazel better. They had something between them that had always eluded Jason. Maybe by getting to know them better, he would have a clearer vision as to how to obtain the level of intimacy with another person that they shared.

Jason left Mike and Hazel's trailer and walked the short distance down to the main office. The back door was still the only access to the building and he entered making his way to the manager's office. He knocked on the door as he walked in, Pam stood up and offered Jason her hand.

They said their hellos, Pam offered him a chair and they both sat down. This was something in the nature of a "get to know you" meeting. They talked for a while discussing where they had been and how it was that they came to be working at the RV park in Yellowstone.

Pam was a retired schoolteacher who had lived in Florida most of her life. She had outlived two husbands. She retired from teaching school for thirty five years and she opened a small store in Texas. A few years later, she sold the store and bought a motor home to start traveling.

Pam was small in stature, barely reaching five feet in height. She had a professional demeanor that was augmented by southern sensibilities and a slight drawl. Life had annealed her eyes with a hardness that spoke of loss and disappointment. She conducted herself in a professional manner and endeavored to project the image of a competent professional administrator. She wore glasses and had her gray hair short. She had given up the effort to appear younger than her years.

As a cashier, Jason needed little supervision after he was trained. Scanning a bar code and making change is about all he had to do. They covered an outline of the training that Jason would receive for his position as a cashier. They briefly visited Jason's responsibilities and work schedule. He was informed of his days off and the assorted benefits of being a campground worker.

It was a short ten minutes of conversation and it was time to go. Pam informed Jason about a general orientation meeting scheduled for the following day. Jason would have the opportunity to meet all the other campground workers at that time. With that information conveyed Jason said his goodbyes and headed back to the bus.

CHAPTER TWELVE
Introduction Meeting

The general introduction meeting was set for ten in the morning. The meeting was held in the lunch room in the main office building. This was the first time that all of the RV park employees had the opportunity to meet all their co-workers. The meeting was like any other first day of a new job meeting. There were rules to go over. You couldn't do this, you must do that, and if you did that it was a sure way to get fired. The senior staff was introduced to all the workers. Pam was known by most and so was Marna, the office manager. Next came the senior guest service agents, the regular agents, the cashiers, and the campground maintenance personnel.

After being informed about the dress code, the code of conduct, and the general hours of operation of the RV park, the employees were dismissed for the day. As everyone was getting up to leave, Stephanie, made an announcement that she intended to drive to Cody and if anybody would like to go to Walmart they were welcome to ride along. Jason spoke up and told Stephanie that he was interested and so did another employee, Tony.

After the meeting ended and the employees talked and milled about the room. Jason watched Stephanie as she talked to another employee. She wore loose fitting clothes that disguised the gentle curves of her figure. Her hair wanted to be blond, but somehow fell just short of the mark and seemed to have a mind of its own. It fought the idea of being combed in any one direction and had a helter skelter look about it. Her complexion was punctuated by a rosy tint to her cheeks that set off her otherwise pale skin. She had blue eyes and stood about five feet eight inches tall and wore braces on her teeth. She looked about the room never really meeting the eyes of the person she was conversing with. Occasionally, she would glance Jason's way, letting him know that she would be there as soon as it was polite to disengage from her conversation.

As she talked, Stephanie would steal glances at Jason. He was tall, well over six feet, with the echo of an athlete's physique, softened by age and a belly that protruded over his belt line. His hair was shoulder length, graying and pulled back into a ponytail and he wore a goatee to mask the slight double chin underneath. He sat waiting in the corner of the room, mostly because the size of the room left him nowhere to go if he got up.

Jason waited until most of the other employees had left before approaching Stephanie about the trip to Cody. They kept the conversation short, both knowing that tomorrow, the long drive would provide the opportunity to talk. A time to meet was set for the following day.

CHAPTER THIRTEEN

Road to Cody

Its twenty seven miles from Fishing Bridge to the east entrance of the park. The road begins with lodge pole pines crowding the road. Just past Pelican Valley and Indian Pond the road opens up and skirts Mary Bay, passing Holmes and Steamboat Point until it reaches Lake Butte Overlook and turns east towards the Park's East entrance. The road climbs between Avalanche and Grizzly Peaks and through Sylvan Pass. From the East entrance its fifty miles to Cody. The road follows Middle Creek as it winds its way down the mountain and to feed into the Buffalo Bill Reservoir, just beyond lies Cody Wyoming.

The road to Cody is where Jason and Stephanie first got to know each other. The Fishing Bridge RV park is in the middle of nowhere. Yellowstone is surrounded on four sides by small towns. Jackson is to the south. West Yellowstone is to the west. Gardiner is to the north and Cody is to the east. The campground was next to Lake Yellowstone near the geographic center of the park. Other concessionaires offered some of the necessities but they were expensive and limited. The truth is, a trip out of the park is required every couple of weeks to get groceries. Cody was where the necessities of life could be purchased.

Stephanie had been in the park for a little over a week. Outside of the training, she had spent much of her time alone. She was eager for the company on the ride down to Cody. Jason had also been in Yellowstone for a week. Jason was not without a vehicle, but it was in need of a little tender loving care. He could benefit from a lift the eighty miles to Cody. He was not low on supplies, but worried that he might not find another way to Walmart in the near future. Jason had arrived on May 1st and the opening date for the campground was May 14th. Jason needed to occupy his time while he waited for the campground to open. The trip to Cody would be a welcome diversion.

Three people were supposed to be on this trip. It turned out that Tony could not go, so it was just Jason and Stephanie. It was a winding road and as this was the first time driving to Cody, it took about an hour and forty five minutes. They were taking in all the sights as they went down the road. The radio was useless, they were way to far from everything to pick up a signal. To pass the time they talked. Stephanie was a southern girl. Jason was also from the south. Being from the South, for Jason there was nothing in the world like the sweet sound of a southern girl's drawl. It was intoxicating. The moment she said hello, Jason was at full attention.

Jason was a little older than Stephanie, she was maybe five or six years younger than him. Stephanie was dressed in clothes that were branded as active and for the outdoors. It was very cold in the park and warm clothes were a necessity. She was wearing hiking boots with a well-insulated jacket and jeans.

Stephanie had a way about her. She was direct and certain in her speech and possessed the voice of a good hearted woman. Traveling down the mountain they introduced themselves. He knew nothing about her and she knew nothing about him. They just started talking about nothing and then they were on to home towns and friends and family. She was from a small town in Tennessee and had lived there her entire life. She was married with one child, a son, who was not planned. Her husband didn't want children and the child came at an inconvenient time. She had him anyway. She was a veterinarian and had started a business that she built into a thriving three vet practice. She had cashed out, selling her business to a large corporation. Her husband was an engineer. He worked for a power company and pushed buttons all day. He had planned to come to Yellowstone with her but changed his mind at the last minute.

As they rode down to Cody and on the return trip, they talked and laughed as they shared moments of their lives. She was a child of German immigrants. Her father was an engineer and her mother a homemaker. Her parents had lived in Germany during World War II and had experienced the harshness of war first hand. After the war, they came to America and her father purchased a small farm. It was an insurance policy for him. The war years had taught him hunger and desperation, the farm was his safety net. He was stern and emotionally distant. Sometimes he treated his children more like farm workers than family members. He stressed education, after all it was education that had saved him. His education allowed him to immigrate to America and make a new life.

Growing up Stephanie felt like an outsider. She was different than the rest of the community. Her mother made all of her clothes. Her mother struggled with English and did not assimilate well into American life. The town Stephanie grew up in had an above average income level and Stephanie felt a little like a duck out of water.

All this did not matter to Stephanie. She did not have time for social non-sense, she was busy. She went to the farm every day after school and worked and in the evening she studied. The next day she got up and did it all over again. Whether it was her way out or just an instilled work ethic, she was determined and had a laser focus on her future.

Stephanie was a force in the universe. She started her own practice very early in her career. She bought a building and converted it into a clinic. Her business continued to grow and she needed to expand. She bought land, designed and built a building and grew it into a three vet practice that employed thirty-five people. At age fifty-two she sold her business to a large corporation. She remained as an employee until a year and a half later when she decided to take a break from her life and explore the world. This is how she made it to Yellowstone.

Stephanie talked about her life and joy, her only son. She glowed when she described him and the various escapades of his youth. He had a gang of friends that she affectionately described as The Locust. They would descend on her house for days on end and would eat everything they could find. Then move to the house of another in the group and repeat the process. He grew up and went to college. This was a turning point for Stephanie. She had invested her life and soul into her son and now he was beginning to live his own life. She had some trouble adjusting.

Stephanie jokingly said she was having a mid-life crisis. She was after all working for minimum wage as a guest service agent. She was nineteen hundred miles from home and living in a trailer park. A couple of times during their conversations it came up that she did not like it when someone played the victim. This got Jason wondering. She was in Yellowstone without her husband, she was not wearing a wedding ring and she was sporting braces on her teeth.

It occurred to Jason that this trip to Cody was a lot like a first date. They had talked for hours, trading stories and opening up to each other. Jason pushed those thoughts out of his mind. She was a married woman and it was going to be a long season. But still, Jason asked himself, was there a message there? A midlife crisis can take many forms. Jason would have to wait and see. The trip to Cody and back ended all too soon for Jason. He had enjoyed the visit with Stephanie. After they returned to the RV park, Jason went his way and Stephanie went hers. It would be several days before they would have time to visit again.

CHAPTER FOURTEEN

Stephanie's Reflections

Dawn lingers in Yellowstone. The mountains on the eastern side of the park block the sun's rays as it appears over the horizon and climbs in the morning sky. Stephanie had a few hours to kill before she was scheduled to start the next training session. She was lying in bed wrapped in layers of blankets, refusing to mentally acknowledge that it was morning and the rest of the world was beginning a new day. She was in a that misty place between sleep and awake and she refused to commit to either. She would watch herself in some long ago memory and rewrite the script. Say the things that she should have said, the words that did not come in time, the answers she could not provide in the heat of the moment, what she wanted to say but couldn't. She imagined another result, a different outcome, a different Stephanie.

She had tried not to allowed the thought to seep into her waking hours, to invade her consciousness. It began while she was sleeping, in her dreams. At first she fought the idea, repulsed by it, frighten by it. As time went by and her unhappiness grew, she acquiesced and allowed herself to daydream. She carried around with her the drugs she used to euthanize pets, enough to end her own life. It was there, in the drawer by the bed, in a small black bag. Everything she needed. It would be simple, no pain, she would just go to sleep and never wake up. An end to the heartache, but what if it was the end, what if there was nothing after, no heaven.

She rolled over clutching an extra pillow to her chest, holding it close, wrapping her arms around it. She fought against the idea. Pushed it from her mind, forced herself to think about something else. Her thoughts turned to the stories she had shared with Jason on their trip to Cody. The stories she had told did not have to be rewritten, they were perfect just as they were. There was no regret, missed opportunities or failing to stand strong for herself. She replayed the stories that Jason had told. She imagined him as a kid and saw him in the neighborhood he lived in, exploring the woods near his house, and the cast of characters that he described. Stephanie imagined herself in those stories and wondered what it would have been like if Jason was a boy down the street and she had know him all her life.

She realized that she had done most of the talking during their drive. But it was more than that, Jason had listened. He was interested and wanted her to talk, wanted her to share her stories. It came to her that for many years, no one had listened, no one had been interested, no one cared what she thought, how she felt, what she worried about. Stephanie rolled over again and went back into the mist, back to the twilight, back to her past.

CHAPTER FIFTEEN

The Circle Of Fire Tour

The park remained blanketed in winter's wonder. With the exception of going out for the occasional work related meeting, Jason stayed holed up in the bus. Most of the other personnel had day long training on the guest registration program. Jason discovered the lending library in the main office building and picked out a couple of books. He spent time going over visitor guides for the park and planning his sightseeing. His days were filled with reading romance novels and taking short walks to acclimate to the altitude. After a few days of staying bundled up inside his bus, Jason was looking forward to the day long employee event scheduled the next day.

In the beginning of the season, activities are offered to all the campground workers. These activities or events occurred prior to the park opening and really have two purposes. They allow everyone to get to know each other and at the same time it exposes them to some of what the park has to offer. This enables the new employees to answer guest questions and help the guest have a better experience in the park.

An example of one of these events or activities is the Circle of Fire Tour. This is a day long bus tour that takes in all of the major attractions in the south end of the park. The south end of the park is where the caldera of the Yellowstone Volcano is located. The Circle of Fire refers to all of the thermal features that can be found at the edge of the caldera.

The tour got off to a rocky start. While driving over to start the tour, the bus driver hit a rock with one of the rear wheels. This put a tear in the sidewall and the tire was losing air. The bus had dual tires on each side of the rear axle but the driver was uncertain as to whether the bus could be operated with only one tire on one side of the rear of the bus. The departure was going to be delayed a bit and the employees waited around for the bus driver to figure it all out.

During the delay everyone was standing in the parking lot next to the bus. People were mingling and mulling around while they waited. Jason took the opportunity to catch up with Stephanie.

"Hey. What's up? Jason began.

"Same routine, computer training all day long." Stephanie answered.

"Got it down yet? Jason asked.

"Are you kidding? I'm not all that computer literate. All the computer stuff was always done for me. This program is hard to learn." Stephanie said.

"You'll get it. Just hang in there." Jason replied.

The bus driver announced that he got the okay to operate the bus with the flat tire and the group started loading the bus. Most of the other employees were married couples and that basically left just Stephanie and Jason as the only singles on the tour. The bus was a forty-five passenger bus and there were twenty employees taking the tour. This left a lot of empty seats. When the time came to load the bus, Stephanie was on the bus first and Jason followed after several other co-workers boarded.

As Jason walked down the aisle he saw Stephanie sitting alone in a row next to a window. She did not look at him as he approached. For a moment he considered sitting down next to her. They had shared a ride to Cody and they were both alone on the trip. He looked for a clue, watching her, hoping she would make eye contact with him as he approached. She was focused on something outside the window. He passed her row and sat two rows back on the opposite side of the bus. Jason wanted the companionship on the tour but she was a married woman and he was a single man. He wasn't sure if she would be comfortable with him planting himself in the seat next to her. He did not get an invitation as he passed her by. He wondered if it was disappointment he saw in her face when he passed her row. It may have just been his imagination.

Yellowstone had not completely opened up and there were still roads that had not been cleared of snow. Normally the Circle of Fire tour makes a complete circle around what is called the lower loop. When the roads through the park were laid out they made what looks like a figure eight. The lower loop includes the Old Faithful area, the Lake Area, the Canyon Junction, Norris, the Madison area, the Fishing Bridge area, the Bridge Bay area and the West Thumb area. The tour was going to visit all these areas except West Thumb. The roads to that part of the park were still closed.

The bus driver finally started the bus and the tour headed out. The driver was much more than a driver, he was an encyclopedia of Yellowstone. This was his tenth year as a tour bus driver. From the moment that the tour began he was on the public address system describing all the history of the park. The first notable place in the park that the bus encountered was the area where it started. Right down the street was a general store, a visitor's center and a car repair garage. As is true in lots of national parks all over the country, buildings like these are more than what they appear. The Visitor's Center and General Store were located in historic log buildings that were constructed in the 1930's. The garage was not simply a garage; it too was an historic building. It was under reconstruction. After being in the environment of Yellowstone for eighty years it was falling down. Committees met and hearings were held identifying historic preservation requirements and after all of that, it was being updated to operate as a garage, but it was being rebuilt to maintain all of the history of the building. These buildings were not open so the bus just drove by and after a description of the history of the area the bus was off to see the Fishing Bridge.

The entire area of the RV Park, Visitor's Center, General Store and Garage is called the Fishing Bridge area. It got this name from the bridge that crossed the Yellowstone River just a hundred or so yards from its mouth at Lake Yellowstone. The bridge is a wood structure with four rows of wooden columns, two rows on each side and logs laid between the rows to form the road bed and walking areas on the bridge. Roy explained that it was first constructed in 1902 and later rebuilt in 1937. The reason that it was called Fishing Bridge was because it was a very popular place to fish. However, fishing is no longer allowed on Fishing Bridge. The part of the Yellowstone River that the bridge crosses is an area that the cut throat trout use for spawning. This is why it is such good fishing from this point. Somehow, someway, nonnative Lake Trout were introduce into Lake Yellowstone and they were eating all the native Cutthroat trout. In order to help save the Cutthroat, fishing from the bridge was banned. It has been a no fishing bridge since 1973.

Stephanie sat looking out the window as the landscape passed by. She was not really paying attention to the tour bus driver. She was miles away, back home, thinking about her life. Remembering her previous trip to Yellowstone and how it had been a bright spot in an otherwise dark and dismal existence. So far, this trip had been a disappointment. She was not reliving a happy moment or any closer to understanding the unhappiness that pervaded her life. She began to question whether she could last out the season.

Leaving the Fishing Bridge area, the bus turned right and headed up the road towards the Canyon Village area. There really isn't much about Yellowstone that does not have some history or other significance attached to it. Heading up the road a short way, the bus came to an area where the Le Hardy Rapids were located. Roy, the tour bus driver informed the group that the rapids were named after Paul Le Hardy, a map maker who, in 1873, encountered the rapids on a raft, capsizing and losing most of his possessions.

The next stop along the Yellowstone River was the Nez Perce Ford. It's now a picnic area but it was a place that the Nez Perce tribe crossed the Yellowstone River in its flight from the U.S. Army in its attempt to reach sanctuary in Canada in 1877.

The Mud Volcano and Sulphur Caldron were next in line. Everyone had to rely on Roy for a description of most of the features at this location. The bus stopped at the Mud Volcano and the group walked up to the features near the parking lot. Snow covered the boardwalks and there was no access to the rest of the features in the Mud Volcano area.

The road continues north and crosses Hayden Valley. According to Roy, the valley was named after Ferdinand Vandeveer Hayden, but no one really knows why. The valley is one of the best places to view wildlife in Yellowstone. It is a vast expanse of grassland that is located mostly to the west of the Yellowstone River between Lake Yellowstone and Canyon Village.

The tour to this point had been sitting in the bus and listening to the wealth of information delivered via the public address system by Roy. The next stop on the tour was the Grand Canyon of the Yellowstone. Jason didn't even know that there was a canyon in Yellowstone, let alone that it was called the Grand Canyon. At the Grand Canyon the group was able to get out of the bus and walk around a bit. The first stop was Artist Point which provides an amazing vista of the lower falls on the Yellowstone. In the background Roy was talking and reciting fact after fact. Jason and Stephanie loosely paired up when they were off the bus. They talked about the views and joked around with the other employees.

Next, the bus drove by Uncle Tom's Cabin trail and Roy explained that Uncle Tom was an early occupant of the park and he built a staircase that allowed guest to walk down into the canyon for a view of the falls. The cabin was gone but the adventurous could still walk down the stair case. That is after the snow melted. Then it was on to the Brink of the Upper Falls. The Yellowstone River has two major water falls within the canyon. The upper falls is the first. This too is a popular tourist stop and the brink of the upper falls is an easy walk.

Everyone piled out of the bus and Jason looked for Stephanie. She was off the bus in a flash and taking in the sights and sounds of the water fall. He hung back for a while making small talk with the other employees on the tour. A part of Jason hoped that she would be interested in paling around together. Jason was a little concerned that he would not have any one to hang out with and Stephanie was about the only candidate for company. But it was more than just a desire for companionship. There was something about Stephanie that drew him to her. Jason liked smart women and Stephanie was indeed smart. He felt drawn to Stephanie and really couldn't describe why.

The Brink of the Upper Falls was just a quick pit stop with a short photo opportunity. It was back in the bus and the day continued with a stop at the Brink of the Lower Falls. The walk to the lower falls was a six hundred foot drop in elevation. The trail led right down to where the water fell over the cliff. At this point, Jason was glad that there was snow all over the trail and it was still closed. The difference in altitude between where Jason was from and Yellowstone was something that he needed to adjust to. Walking around the RV Park Jason would get out of breath walking on flat ground. He couldn't imagine how hard it would be to walk back up six hundred feet in elevation on that trail.

Inspiration Point was next and then it was on to Canyon Village. Yellowstone has major hubs with visitor's centers and campgrounds or lodging for Park visitors. Canyon Village is one of these hubs. The area includes a campground, a lodge, a general store, a visitor's center, a couple of restaurants and employee housing. The entire area had not yet opened. The doors to the visitor's center were open and there was access to the restrooms, but that was about it. The group walked around looking at the area for a few minutes and then headed off to the next stop.

The Norris and Madison campgrounds were closed so it was a quick drive through and then on to the thermal features in the Norris Geyser Basin just above Old Faithful. The group was able to do a couple of short walks around boardwalks in the geyser basin. It seemed that the sights to see were endless. Finally the tour ended up at Old Faithful. The bus was stopping for lunch so that the employees could eat at the employee dining hall. It was a family style affair with everyone sitting around a large table making small talk and getting to know each other. The visitor's center at Old Faithful was open and the group made the tour. Finally it was time to go to the observation area and witness Old Faithful erupt. Then it was back on the bus. The final leg of the loop was closed so the bus had to retrace its steps to return to the Fishing Bridge area. Since this was just a bus ride everyone started asking questions of the guide. In the beginning the questions were serious and the answers were very informative on the nature of the park. Then they turned silly. Someone asked when the alligators came out of their dens on the Yellowstone River and it was downhill from there. It turned into a very funny question and answer period. Finally the bus returned to the campground and everyone headed home for the day.

CHAPTER SIXTEEN

Opening Day Jason

The park opened on a Friday and it was all hands on deck. Jason had received his one half hour training on the cash register and was ready to begin his career as a cashier. Stephanie and the rest of the customer service agents completed their two-week training on the computer program. The campground attendants had completed all the necessary tasks to open the park to visitors. Snow was still everywhere. The campground guests had to park in between the wall of white, in spaces that have been plowed open. Everyone was feeling their way as they went. When Jason arrived to begin his shift, he looked for Stephanie, she was not there. He checked the work schedule and discovered that she was not working until the following day.

The front door of the main office opened up to the reservations area. This was a lobby with a large counter on one side of the room. The guest service agents were lined up in a row behind this counter with the cashier at one end. For most of the day, all the guest service agents had to do was stand in front of their computer terminals with their hands propped against the counter waiting for a guest to arrive so that they could be registered.

The main building contained the registration area, a gift shop, an activities center, a laundry, and shower facilities. Jason was a cashier and responsible for selling products in the gift store and supervising the laundry. His laundry duties included making change and insuring that the machines were not abused. He also was responsible for the showers. Guests who stayed at the RV Park received free showers and everyone else had to pay. Jason was the gate keeper.

The day went by without much in the way of problems. Most everybody on duty that day was a first season employee of the park so this was their first day too. The traffic in and out of the campground was minimal. Two kinds of guest came to the park, walk ins and those with reservations. The ones with reservations were easy. All of their information was in the computer system already and mostly all that was required was to collect their money and explain about the bears. The walk ins required a little more time. All of their information had to be entered into the computer.

And then there were the questions. What to see first and what not to miss. Most of the guest were driving tourist. They wanted to ride around in their cars and drive up to the site to see. Or maybe just a short walk. Everyone had been on the Circle of Fire Tour and had some idea of how to answer these questions.

The park was still snow bound and there were only a few visitors on this first day. Jason had a very slow day. He sold twenty seven dollars' worth of merchandise during the seven hours that he acted as a cashier. Jason had lots of time on his hands to meet and talk with his fellow worker.

The campground had a policy of allowing couples to work together. This allowed for time off together so that the couples could explore the park. On this particular day the staff included Mike and Hazel and Gordon and Betty. Mike, Hazel and Betty were all guest service agents and Gordon was their supervisor, a senior agent. Jason had already met Mike and Hazel. This was the first time he had the opportunity to spend time with Gordon and Betty.

Gordon and Betty were full time RVers. They had owned their own business and sold it fifteen years before coming to the park. During that time they traveled around the country exploring

America. Over the course of the fifteen years their funds began to deplete. During the first part of their travels they mostly volunteered at various parks and recreation centers. Eventually they had to begin supplementing their resources by working for periods of the year. This was why they had chosen to come to Yellowstone this year.

Shelly and Jim stopped in during the first day. They were a couple and working at the RV Park for the season. They had limped their way to Yellowstone in a beat up 1975 camper. Jim had been given the camper by a friend and he had made it usable as a living space for the season in Yellowstone.

Shelly was a twenty-two year old free spirit who was in Yellowstone because she was in love with Jim. She wore short brown hair and had tattoos on various parts of her body. One in particular was leopard spots that started somewhere above her shoulder and continued down her arm to just above the elbow. Five foot six and slender, her ears had multiple piercings but on this occasion, she only wore one pair of ear rings. At first glance Shelly seemed vapid and unrefined. Her appearance did not tell the whole story. She had grown up in the high desert of California where she completed high school and went to cosmetology school. It had always been her dream to learn how to cut hair and she started working in the local salons and then moved to Boston to work. She felt out of place in the big city and returned home within a year. Shelly was a vast reservoir of untapped abilities. Her family did not focus on education. She was capable of doing anything that she set her mind to but had never been inspired to reach for any lofty goals. After returning from Boston, she met Jim.

Jim was in the desert living with band mates exploring his creativity and playing music at local bars and parties. Jim was the lead singer and the writer of all of the bands materials. Jim was older, about thirty four, but looked younger than his age. He wore his clothes tight. It seemed that everything he wore was one or two sizes too small. He was always in a ball cap that disguised the utter lack of hair on top of his head. Jim stood just under six foot tall and had a trim muscular body.

Eventually the first day ended and no major disasters occurred. It was time to close up. Everyone went their separate ways. Jason headed back to the bus and settled in to making dinner. He was exhausted from the day's work. The altitude was something he definitely needed to get used to. Jason turned in for the night. The next day he was up again and back at his station as a cashier. The routine had begun.

CHAPTER SEVENTEEN
Opening Day Stephanie

Stephanie's first day of work was a day after the park opened. She began her day at eight in the morning, at her station behind the counter in the campground's main building. The doors opened and no one came in. It was a little anticlimactic, two weeks of waiting and no one showed up. As the day progressed, guest started trickling in. Three other reservation agents were on duty with Stephanie and it catch as catch can. Someone would walk through the door and everyone would say hello and try and strike up a conversation.

Guest service agents were responsible for registering guests and seeing to their needs. Two classes of employees handled these responsibilities, guest service agents and senior guest service agents. The regular guest service agents would do the check-ins. The campground was a part of the park and owned by the government. The National Park Service required the campground to inform guests of the rules of the park. Most of the rules centered on grizzly bears and how to stay out of trouble with these bears.

Stephanie had seen a grizzly bear in the wild and she had read about bear safety in the visitor's guides she devoured while waiting for the park to open. Most grizzly bears hibernate at about the same altitude in the mountains. The RV Park was located at this altitude. In addition, there was a long valley with south facing slopes that was just east of the park. Just west of the park was wintering grounds for the herd animals of Yellowstone. Bears prefer south facing slopes when choosing a den site. The sun hits the south facing slopes the earliest in the season. In reality, the RV Park is located on a well-used route from a major denning area to a major dining area for bears. Most of the check in process was a lecture on how to stay bear safe. Everything that was said to a registering guest was required by the National Park Service. Most of the information told to registering guest centered around the Grizzly Bears in the park.

Stephanie listened to the canned speech each reservation agent was required to give to all arriving campers. The first thing an agent told a registering guest was that the campground was for hard sided vehicles only. Tents of any kind were not allowed. If a camper had a pop up trailer, he could not stay in the RV park. This rule was instituted by the Park Service because bears are very smart. If they associate food with anything they would remember it always. Tents are easy for a bear to get into; so no tents.

Campers could not leave any food outside or anything that was used to cook food. Coolers had to be stored indoors and pets could not be left tied up outside. Bears and other predators would attack and kill a pet tied up to an RV. Finally the Park Service recommended that guests always walk around in groups of three and carry bear spray.

Stephanie projected down the road a month or two and imagined what it would be like to have listened to and given this speech day after day. In no time at all she would begin incoherently babbling the bear mantra. She asked herself if she could do this day after day until the end of the season. There was still a chance that her husband would come and join her. It was too soon to make any decisions. Maybe she needed some time alone anyway.

CHAPTER EIGHTEEN

The Brink of the Upper Falls

Winter lingers in Yellowstone and it does not take long to appreciate that there are only two seasons, winter and July. It was early June and the campground had been opened two weeks. It had snowed three times during that period. The day time highs had threatened sixty degrees on a couple of days. At night, the temperature would dip down below zero. The winter was slowly receding, especially in the areas where the ray of the sun could reach the ground. The Park Service was actively clearing obstructions from some of the more popular and accessible trails.

Jason's work week began on Thursday and continued until Monday. He had Tuesdays and Wednesdays off and after checking the schedule he learned that Stephanie had Monday and Tuesdays off. Everyone shared an eagerness to get out and explore the park. Jim and Shelly most likely would become Stephanie's hiking companions as they too were off on Mondays and Tuesdays. On their first day off together, they were off on a hike and exploring the park.

Stephanie, Shelly and Jim returned from their excursion and stopped by the main building giving everyone a rundown of where they had been. As it turned out, Jim and Shelly had plans for the following day and that left Stephanie without a hiking partner. Jason took the opportunity to make plans to meet up with Stephanie the following day and go exploring.

Stephanie had visited the park in the past as a tourist. She was familiar with the highlights that someone would see who was only in the park for a few days. She suggested that they head up through the Hayden Valley to the waterfalls on the Yellowstone River. One of the first places Jason had seen in the park was the Grand Canyon of the Yellowstone and that is where the waterfalls were on the Yellowstone River. On the Circle of Fire Tour, the trail down into the canyon was covered with snow and ice. Word came that the trail down to the Upper and Lower Falls had been cleared and were now open.

The Upper Falls marked the beginning of the Grand Canyon of the Yellowstone. The canyon is an amazing feature that winds its way for twenty miles through the park. It is a thousand feet deep in places and it all begins at the upper falls. The canyon hugs the side of the Washburn Mountain Range as the Yellowstone River snakes its way north and west until it exits the park at Gardiner. The Brink of the Upper Falls trail is a short walk that leads down to an observation point right at the edge of the falls. From this point it is possible to look over the edge and watch the water tumble one hundred feet to the rocks below.

A short ways up the road from the Upper Falls is that trail to the brink of the Lower Falls. This trail descends six hundred feet by way of a number of switch backs. The walk to the end of the trail is only a short half mile down and leads to an observation point that allows hikers to gaze over a precipice and view the Yellowstone River tumbling three hundred and eight feet as it continues its journey into the Canyon.

Stephanie and Jason played tourist marveling at the sheer power of the water as it fell from the cliff. Jason's eyes followed the water as it approached the point of no return, then tumbled into the abyss far below. The view inspired both awe and fear at the power and danger present in the falls. In a place like this with the grandeur of the canyon and the power of the water, a person can't help but feel insignificant.

The mist from the falls rose up from the depths and

surrounded them. It gave them a chill and they decided to start their return trip to the parking lot. Jason was overweight and out of shape. He was completely out of breath before they reached the first turn of a switchback. Fortunately for him, the park service had the foresight to put a bench at the turn for every switchback. He was so out of shape, he had to stop and rest at each bench. It was a little humbling for Jason. Especially since Stephanie was in excellent physical condition. Stephanie was a girl and she was kicking his butt all over this hike. Jason had not eliminated all the macho feelings that society had instilled in him.

The thing about walking and being out of breath is that it is impossible to talk. That meant that Jason had to get Stephanie to do all the talking. Even after they made it to the next bench, it took him several minutes to get his breath back. All he could do was just listen. She was very gracious not chastising him for being out of shape. She talked about her work and the people that worked with her. She continued to tell him the story of her life, but not in any organized way. She was remembering her childhood and growing up in a small southern town. Jason had grown up in a small southern town, but he had left for a big city out west. She had stayed home and had lived all her life in a town with less than ten thousand people.

Stephanie's stories had a familiarity to them. Jason could relate in a way that only someone who had lived in a small southern town could. He listened and reminisced as he tried to catch his breath. Her stories took him back to his childhood, his little neighborhood and to the long summer days that Jason wished would never end.

Jason would catch his breath and continue the climb to the top, walking to the next switch back and again, he would need to rest. Stephanie kept him entertained. He sat listening enthralled and gasping for breath. Every now and then he would be able to manage a question or two. His questions had one purpose, to keep Stephanie talking.

When they made the top of the third switch back, he again

had to sit down. Stephanie began telling a story about her father. She had told Jason that her father and mother were German immigrants that had moved here after World War II. That he was an engineer and that he had a career in manufacturing.

"My father is a very unusual man. He never throws away anything." Stephanie began. "He's eighty-seven years old and he thinks nothing of stopping as he drives along and picking something out of the trash. I have to be careful about my garbage. If I throw away a vacuum cleaner, he will take it out of the trash and take it to his farm. You should see his barn. It is full of useless stuff that he refuses to throw away. He had an old beat up crashed truck that was from the 1960's that he keeps there. When I was a kid, he backed the truck into a tree to tear off all the doors. The seats have completely decayed and all that is left is the wire seat springs."

Jason detected a little embarrassment in Stephanie's voice. She was telling him a story but at the same time she was sort of apologizing for her father. This made Jason wonder if in fact she had felt the same way when she was young. Fitting in is very important in grade school. Having parents that are distinctly different from everyone else can be a source of concern when trying to fit in and be like everyone else. Jason continued to listen as she continued to describe the antics of her father.

"The clinic was a social outlet for him. He loved teasing the staff and playing the role of everyone's grandpa. He is the sort of person that would hang a paper towel up to dry so that he could reuse it later. He also has absolutely no filter whatsoever. He will say whatever crosses his mind. I can't tell you how many times I've had to scold him after he made a comment about the personal appearance or the weight of one of the employees at the clinic. "

Stephanie was not at a loss for stories. One switch back after another she related stories about clinic workers and clients. There was the man with all the cats and the story of the lady with more dogs than she could count. Stephanie's favorite stories were about the cast of characters that work at the clinic. It was like she was the mother hen to all the staff and took great delight in their antics. The Clinic had thirty five full time employees and over the years there were countless others that had come and gone. Jason listened, grateful for the fact that there were stories to tell. Grateful that he didn't have to talk.

As she talked, Stephanie kept going over in her mind her reasons for coming to Yellowstone. She had wanted to clear the deck and get a new perspective on her life. She was not happy and wanted to understand what was driving her feelings. On this hike she had recounted happy memories of her life back home. She was laughing and smiling as she told her stories. She was having a good time and was enjoying Jason's company.

They eventually made it back to the top of the canyon rim. They got back in the car and drove up the rest of the way to Canyon Village, just sightseeing and talking. Canyon Village is one of several hubs around Yellowstone. The Village has a Visitor's Center, a campground, a gas station, a general store, lodging for guests and a few other amenities. They did not stop at the Village. The ride back to the campground was quieter. Jason was worn out by the effort of climbing out of the canyon. It is about fifteen miles between Canyon Village and the Fishing Bridge area. Although it is only fifteen miles it takes between forty-five minutes to an hour to make the drive. The road winds along at times following the Yellowstone River and at times crossing the wide open expanse of Hayden Valley. The Hayden Valley was a vast expanse of white. Off in the distance, they would occasionally see dark specks on the crests of hills. The specks were bison that knew to stay in the wind blown areas where the covering was not as deep.

As they drove, Jason looked back, into his past and the road that had brought him to Yellowstone. Listening to Stephanie's stories had resurrected memories that he had not visited in years. He felt it odd that he was in a wondrous place for the first time and he was at the same time traveling back in time to memories long forgotten.

59

"I'm having a midlife crisis, what brought you here?" Stephanie asked.

"I just wanted a simpler life." Jason began. "I sort of dropped out."

"Dropped out?" Stephanie asked.

"You're too young to remember the sixties. That was a phrase back then. Drop out. It means leaving the rat race." Jason explained.

"I just came to believe that I was not running my own life, it was running me." Jason said. "A person can be a prisoner of his possessions. A prisoner of their own life. I decided that I wanted to be the author of my own story.

"So, you dropped out? Stephanie asked.

" I had a mortgage, car payments, credit card payments and of course the water and lights. I could not stop working. Every month there was another payment due. I had to get up, go to work and make money to pay for it all. I had no choice. "

" So that's what you mean by "a prisoner of your possessions? Stephanie asked.

"Yeah. I had a thirty-five hundred square foot house. It had three bedrooms and a den. I never went into most of the house. I only used three rooms; the den, the bedroom and the bathroom, that was it. I ate out three meals a day. It was never ending. "

"So, what did you do?" Stephanie asked.

"Finally, I decided that I had had enough. I sold the big house and moved into a small two bedroom house. It was only eight hundred and fifty square feet and it was still too big. I never went into the spare bedroom. But that was okay, I went from a thirty-five hundred dollar monthly mortgage to only eight hundred a month. I got rid of his pricey car and picked up a nice used one with no monthly payments. I stopped eating at fancy restaurants and ate at home more often. I wanted to live simpler. I down sized my life. "

"I just kept downsizing until there was only the bus and car."

60

Jason began. "It took some time, but I sold my house and everything in it. Got rid of the expensive car and started living the life of a gypsy. I got stuck a couple of times, but I'm wandering around now. "

Stephanie listened and reflected on her own decision to come to Yellowstone. She had a lot in common with Jason. She too felt that her life was out of her control. She wanted a new way of living. The conversation drifted off and they both sat and looked at the wonders of Yellowstone. They navigated passed a buffalo jam in the Hayden Valley before they reached the campground and said good night.

CHAPTER NINETEEN
The Lone Wolf

Lynn lived full time in Cody, about eighty miles to the east of the Fishing Bridge RV park. She had been a devoted fan of Yellowstone all of her life. Lynn had worked at the campground for six consecutive years and was a true veteran at the campground. In her mid-sixties, she had lived a lifetime as a long-haul trucker prior to retirement. It was her and her husband as a driving team. Her husband had passed away and now she was left on her own. Lynn's answer to keeping herself busy was devoting herself to Yellowstone and her love for wolves. If anyone had any questions about any aspect of the park or the services available to guest, Lynn was the source to seek for answers.

Lynn had long ago lost her battle in the war to resist eating comfort food. She had become resigned in the idea and accepting of the fact that she was and would remain overweight. This however was not much of a hindrance to Lynn. She was out walking around the park, binoculars in hand, trying to get glimpses of the wolf packs that haunted the Lamar and Hayden Valleys. There was no better ambassador to the wonders that are Yellowstone than Lynn. She was truly and genuinely interested in extending her wonder and devotion and enhancing in any way possible the experience of Yellowstone for the guests of the RV park.

For most of the day, Stephanie would sit on her stool watching the ebb and flow of campers coming in and out of the park. She had nothing much to do except wait for someone who wanted to check into the campground. Lynn occupied a small office on the other side of the reservation counter. It was semi-private and allowed the Senior Guest Service Agents a little quiet as they moved around reservations to fill as much of the parks campsites as possible. Stephanie would wander down the counter and stand in the door to talk to Lynn.

Lynn had the patience to allow each of the reservation agents to come to proficiency on the computer in their own time. It was easier for some than others. Lynn was equally supportive of each and everyone. Stephanie understood this quality in Lynn and admired it. Stephanie had countless employee come through her clinic and could appreciate how hard it was to not get frustrated when someone was not picking up on what they needed to know.

Lynn was lonely and it was plain for anyone to see. She had not planned to live her golden years alone. She had lived a lifetime in the companionship of her husband. A husband and wife long-haul trucker team spend a lot of time together. They had met in their twenties and had been married almost forty years. He got sick suddenly and she lost him in what seemed to her a heartbeat. She was at a time and place where finding another was not in the cards.

Lynn turned to lost and stray souls, who became her constant companions. She had a large house in Cody and she had numerous house guests. Not guests in the traditional sense, these guests were the disconnected, living from day to day souls that populate the edge of mainstream life. Those people who were perpetually getting their lives together. Lynn's house was a respite on their journey. For some its dogs or cats, for Lynn it was people. There was always room for another.

Stephanie saw a little of herself in Lynn. She had not planned to live alone in the autumn of her life. She wanted a life companion, but like Lynn, Stephanie had come to question if that was in the cards. Lynn had been alone for a number of years and although she occupied her life with activities, her loneliness was palpable. Meeting Lynn caused Stephanie to pause. Lynn was a genuine, kind, and goodhearted person making the best of what had happened to her while she was making other plans. She had built a busy life that was full of temporary connections with other people. Her house guests would wander in and out of her life. Her home was a way station on their journey. She worked in a campground in a National Park where there was a constant turnover of guests. Even her fellow employees were just passing through, working for the season and then on to their next adventure. Stephanie was one of these temporary characters in the constant parade that passed by Lynn.

Stephanie wanted to change her life and she was constantly wondering why she felt that way. Her practice, her husband, her house, and everything else that went with them were all part of he mix. Stephanie wanted to escaped the sadness, the chains and be unencumbered. Lynn had brought into focus an issue that Stephanie needed to reconsider. Stephanie was following a path that would disconnect her from her life and family. She needed to decide if she could really travel this road alone and be truly happy.

.

CHAPTER TWENTY

The Social Director

Marna was the office manager of the campground and the second in command. She was the better half of a couple working at the campground. Her other half was Bob who worked as a campground attendant. During the first week of working in the campground Jason got to know them both. Jason did not have a busy work life. He sat behind the counter and waited for someone to buy something. Jason was almost always available to talk with another campground employee. This is where Jason got to know Marna and Bob.

Marna was fun loving, energetic and in everyone's business. She was a competent capable person and cared deeply about providing a good experience to the campground guest. Marna was the unofficial social director for the work crew. She was genuinely concerned that the campground workers had a good experience while working at the park. Marna would cook breakfast for the crew or arrange a cookout in honor of whatever holiday was on the calendar. Marna believed that part of the reason that the workers were at the camp ground was to have fun. She wanted to have fun and she wanted everyone else to have fun with her.

She had her thyroid removed and that resulted in her being slightly overweight. Although she had a few extra pounds she wore them very well. She was rounded and curvy in all the right places. Marna understood that most of the campground employees had had long professional careers and did not require micromanagement in the task they were assigned.

She was married to Bob who was fifteen years her senior. Bob was a retired police officer and an avid car collector. Bob was truly a nice guy who was there to support his wife in her efforts to have adventures in their golden years. Bob was a no nonsense kind of guy. He would not sugar coat it when he had something to say. He would just say it like it was. He did not have time for the petty politics of the campground staff.

Marna worked in the back office where Jason had first met Pam. She and Pam worked opposite each other. When Pam was there, Marna was off. When Marna was there it was Pam's turn to be off. As it turned out, Marna was on duty for most of Jason's shifts.

Marna had never had children. She turned her mothering instinct towards her two dogs and everyone that worked in the campground. Within the first week working at the campground, Marna had a schedule of all of the employee potlucks posted on the bulletin board. When she worked the opening shift, she would bake cinnamon rolls or make pigs in a blanket for everyone to enjoy. Jason took an immediate liking to Marna.

CHAPTER TWENTY-ONE
Grizzly

It was a short half mile walk down to Fishing Bridge. The area was still not completely open. The Visitor's Center and the General Store were still closed. The park service had cleared the path from the RV park down to the general store. From the store to just short of the bridge, it was parking lots that had also been cleared. The last one hundred yards was along the side of the road, between the pavement and the snow banks.

It was still very cold in Yellowstone. The cold moist wind fought its way pasted Jason's collar and burnt against his cheeks. The Yellowstone River was free of ice and flowed flat and calm on both sides of the bridge. Ice ringed the lake and snow covered the banks and everything else.

Jason and Stephanie made it to the bridge and began taking photographs. The landscape sloped down to the bridge from both sides and the banks were covered with trees to the river's edge. On the far side of the bridge there was a small empty parking lot and woods on both sides of the road. They crossed the bridge taking photos along the way. When they got to the opposite side of the bridge they turned around and took shots from that perspective.

Jason took photographs of the bridge, the upstream approach, and downstream view, then began to walk back towards the center of the bridge. They was just taking his time and enjoying the moment. Jason stood looking over the railing, peering into the water, searching for signs of life. Stephanie had lagged behind and was focused on getting a photograph of Lake Yellowstone and the mountains beyond.

As Jason was standing there, taking in all the breathtaking views that is Yellowstone National Park, he noticed some movement about one hundred and fifty yards up the road towards the campground. He looked a little closer and realized that a grizzly bear was walking down the center of the road. The bear was headed straight for the bridge. Jason yelled at Stephanie.

"Hey, come here." Stephanie heard the stress in his voice and walked over.

"What' up?

Pointing back toward the RV park, Jason just said, "bear."

Stephanie stared for a moment and recognized the lumbering brown mass coming down the road.

"Oh God, what are we going to do?"

Jason stopped to consider his options. If they walked towards the bear, they may be able to get off of the bridge. The problem with that was that there was only woods to both the right and left of the road. There was a chance that the bear would not cross the bridge and instead turn off the road and head into the woods. If they went in the opposite direction and crossed the bridge to the bank behind them, there were woods on both sides of the road for approximately a half a mile up to its intersection with the Grand Loop road.

"We have no place to go." He said. He watched as the bear walked down the road closing the distance. Jason hoped that the bear would turn off of the road and follow the bank of the river. They were not so lucky. The bear kept coming and walked right onto the bridge.

Jason's thoughts turned to Stephanie. Jason was standing next to the edge of the bridge looking over into the water and wondering just how cold that water might be. They had only one alternative if they were to get in trouble with the grizzly, and that was to jump off the bridge into the water.

"Can you swim?" he asked.

Stephanie turned and look at him, making the connections. She knew that there was no way of getting off the bridge. They were going to have a close encounter with a grizzly bear and there was no way to avoid it.

"That will be the last resort, if the bear gets aggressive, we jump." Jason continued. "Stay behind me. Don't make any fast movements, and what every you do, don't run. It's only thirty yards to the shore. We can make it. The currents not that strong and we will end up, just down the bank."

Stephanie stood looking around, trying to find another escape path. As they stood there watching the bear approach, a pickup truck came down the road from behind them, pulling up and stopping about three quarters of the way across the bridge.

Jason tried to get the attention of the driver and get in the truck. The pickup had a couple of dogs inside and they were going crazy barking at the bear. There was no way that the driver could hear Jason yelling at him. Jason decided that their best course of action was to keep the pickup truck between them and the bear. Jason watched the bear as it walked on the bridge and kept the truck aligned so that it was at all times between him and the bear.

Stephanie stayed close behind Jason, pressed up against his back and slightly to the side. Just enough to see what was going on. Jason felt behind him with his left arm, finding the edge of Stephanie's body, and held his right arm up to hold her behind him.

Jason hoped that the bear would not notice them and keep walking across the bridge. This strategy worked until the bear was even with the pickup truck. They were on one side, the bear was on the other, and the pickup truck was in the middle. Jason yelled at the driver not to move. The driver did not hear him yell.

Without any warning, the pickup truck began to leave. It pulled away while the bear was directly across the bridge from Jason and Stephanie. The bear looked over at Jason and Jason looked at him. The grizzly opened his mouth, showing his teeth. Jason pushed back moving Stephanie towards the bridge railing. Stephanie was halfway up the railing on the side of the bridge waiting to see what was going to happen next. The bear turned his head back in the direction of his travel and just kept on walking crossing the bridge and disappearing into the woods on the other side. Jason and Stephanie made their way back to the campground a little shaken up. They really didn't believe what had just happened but they had a great story to tell the other campground workers.

Within the confines of Yellowstone National Park there are somewhere in the neighborhood of nine hundred Grizzly Bears. Seeing a Grizzly Bear is the crowning event for most visitors to the park. They are majestic animals that inspire awe and reverence in anyone who encounters one. A Grizzly bear can weigh up to eight hundred pounds. The average bear is six and a half feet in length. They are normally dark brown in color, but can range from light cream to black. They can be distinguished from a Black Bear by their concave faces and the hump on their back at the shoulders. They have long claws up to four inches. The Grizzly Bear's guard hairs usually have white tips, giving them a grizzled appearance from which they get their name. They are omnivores eating seeds, berries, roots, grasses, fungi, deer, elk, fish, dead animals and insects. Jason heard himself saying, "Thank goodness we were not on the menu."

CHAPTER TWENTY-TWO

The days started blending

The days started blending into each other as routine set in and the countless faces that appeared at the counter came and went in an endless procession. The RV parks guests where from every corner of America and every part of the world. Stephanie's favorite part of the job was helping guests plan their visit to the park. Her responsibilities including selling tickets to the tours and activities around Yellowstone. There was a boat tour of the lake, a chuck wagon excursion and a photo tour where an old Yellow Bus from the 1930's hauls the visitors around the park to the most scenic sites. Ranger talks, Ranger walks and the Visitor Centers were free and a great way to experience and learn about the park. Stephanie enjoyed helping a visitor get the most out of the their days in the park.

Stephanie was glad to have a hiking partner in Jason. Her husband's last minute change of plans never gave her the opportunity to consider the possibility that it would be hard to find companionship for her explorations. Jason was in a similar situation needing and wanting company as he explored the park. Stephanie was a little concerned about the amount of time that she and Jason were spending together. It was a small group and people love to talk. If she wanted a hiking partner, she had no other choice.

Stephanie found herself watching Jason on the days when they shared the same shifts. She could see that Jason's enjoyed the constant parade of faces that passed in front of him. He would strike up conversations with anyone and everyone. He was a people person and loved interacting with the Parks guest. People from all over the world came to Yellowstone. India was very well represented in the guest population. Guests from China, Europe, Africa, and the Middle East all came through the gift shop and wanted souvenirs of their visit. Jason talked to them all.

Stephanie like to watch how Jason interacted with the children that came into the campground. Jason particularly liked talking to the young children. He would asked about what animals they had seen and about the water that would shoot up out of the ground. He loved listening to them describe in wonder the strange happening they witnessed and the animals that they saw. It was obvious to her that he loved children and was very good with them.

One day a particular little girl came into the office and Jason struck up a conversation with her. She could not have been more than four years old. Stephanie listened as she talked about her experiences around the park. After describing all the sights she had seen and the animals she had encountered, Jason asked her what she wanted to be when she grew up. Without missing a beat she shook her head and said "I'm not going to grow up." Jason laughed and agreed that if he had the choice he would not grow up either.

Stephanie's husband would never have a conversation with a four year old. He didn't want children and was angry when she got pregnant. She tried to imagine what her life would have been like without her son. The fact was beginning to sink in, she would never have stayed married to her husband if it was not for their son.

One of Stephanie's reasons for this trip was to clear the board, to eliminate all the stress out of her life and find the source of her unhappiness. She had refused to allow herself to think about the constant need to end the life of a pet and whether it had any part in the way she felt. In the days before she left when she was still working, she was like a robot, getting to the clinic early and working until late at night. She was spending most of her down time alone and sleeping. Her husband worked the evening shift and she only saw him on the evenings of his days off. She had lost interest in everything and everybody. Her son was off living his own life and she barely talked to him. An hour or two every few weeks when he would come up for air and actually call her from where ever he was in the universe. He had quit school and was working seasonal jobs around the country. A camp counselor in Maine or a wilderness tour guide in North Carolina were just a couple of the jobs that he said kept him away from cell service.

Stephanie was almost completely cut off from her old life. Calling out, back to civilization was hard in Yellowstone. There was no cell phone coverage and that was just fine with Stephanie. She had been the solution to everyone's problems at the clinic. Even after she sold out and there was conflict, she was expected to fix whatever was wrong. Whenever she would get within cell range, she would check her messages and they were mostly clinic workers complaining about something or other. She refused to call them back. She was done playing nursemaid to all of other employees. Everything else considered, she still kept coming back to compassion fatigue. She knew that she would have to confront the questions soon.

CHAPTER TWENTY-THREE
The Professor and His Student

Over the next few days Stephanie worked with Jim and Shelly several days in a row. Business was still very slow and she got the opportunity to get to know them better. Their relationship was one of mentor and student. Jim was the tortured artist and she was the willing student. Jim was the product of a broken home and his mother had contracted a fatal disease and had died when he was eighteen. His father was an alcoholic and general ne'er-do-well. He had been forced to grow up faster than most and the responsibility and loss had its effect upon him. The impact of the loss of his mother was palpable. Stephanie could see it in Jim's mannerism and hear it in his voice. Jim wore it for anyone to see and it was present in all his music. Jim was also a very capable person who had failed to tap into all his potential. He had no college education and was a self-taught musician. Jim seemed to feel his feeling deeper than the average person. Perhaps it was the lost of his mother at an early age, but for whatever the reason he seemed more passionate, more sensitive and more pensive than most.

They had arrived in a 1975 class C motor home that had seen its better days. It was small by comparison to what everyone else drove but it could accommodate a loving couple. Jim was a very talented musician.   The problem with being a musician is that it can be really hard to make any money.

Shelly was not accustomed to being treated well. Shelly had missed these lessons in life. She did not expect any of these things and was taken aback when on the first occasion that they went to Cody together Jason opened the truck's door for her. This caught Stephanie's attention. Jim did not demonstrate these traits. He was not a person that opened doors for anyone. He had trouble seeing past his own needs and freely caring for and respecting others was not in his nature. It was not that he was mean or uncaring. It was that he had been through a lot when he was young and it was as if he was saying, "no one showed me much concern when I was going through my troubles. No one opened any doors for me, why should I open any doors for anyone else?" Shelly on the other hand had a loving caring intact family. She was incapable of seeing the flaws in Jim's personality and accepted him as he was.

There was heartbreak written into their relationship and it was only a matter of time before it would rise to the surface. Jim wanted to brood and focus on the harshness of life. Shelly just wanted to have fun. The leader of the band may be alluring and romantic when in an environment that lends status to this position. In Yellowstone, there were no bars or nightspots and Jim was just another worker bee at the campground. Maybe that special magic possessed by lead singers was destine to fade, but Jason believed that it would not be long before conflict ensued.

Stephanie took an immediate liking to Shelly. She could see with absolute certainty the mistakes that Shelly was going to make and was certain that she could steer her to safety. It was more than an expression of a mothering instinct. Stephanie saw her own mistakes when she looked at Shelly. If only someone had taken the time to help her, to guide her, she would not have spent the last decade in a failed marriage. Stephanie was going to take Shelly under her wing and help her make better decisions.

CHAPTER TWENTY-FOUR
The Odd Couple

Dale was a retired manager for the department store J.C. Penny. He had worked in retail for forty years. Joyce was a registered nurse and had ended up specializing in addiction recovery. The two of them were high school sweethearts and had been married all of their lives. They were devoted to each other. Dale was a tall man, at least six foot five inches tall. Joyce on the other hand was petite, barely over five feet tall. They were very traditional and conservative and placed family above everything. They too had recently retired, but they were too busy to sit at home and watch TV. They had a pull behind trailer and were intent on traveling the country. They didn't need to work at the park to afford to be there, they just wanted the experience.

Dale at first was constantly baiting Jason with insults. Bantering back and forth, insulting each other is not an uncommon occurrence between male friends. But this was different. His comments included a subtext, a level of hostility. It reminded Jason of what it was like when he was young and he would meet someone in the world that disapproved of the length of his hair or the way he dressed. They would not overtly insult him, but they would announce their disapproval of him with subtle mannerisms. It was one of those things that is hard to explain. It was hard to point to any one thing, but Dale had an air about him that conveyed a feeling of condemnation. This was Dale in the beginning. Later Jason learned that when Dale first saw him, he judged him as a low life and that he had been in error. Dale admitted that he was glad that he did not let his first impression control the rest of their interactions.

Joyce on the other hand was as close to an angel on earth as any person Jason had ever met. She did not have a mean bone in her body. She is a forgiving soul, with a charity of understanding. A person could bare their sins to Joyce and know that understanding and forgiveness were a certainty. Joyce was all about family. Family was the most important thing in the universe.

Joyce was a fellow cashier and Dale worked as a campground attendant. Because Joyce was a cashier, it took a while for Jason to get to know her. Only one cashier was on duty at any given time. Jason tried to spend most of his off time out in the park. The only time that Jason got to see Joyce was during shift changes. Eventually, Jason needed to do laundry and Joyce was on duty. While he waited for his clothes to wash and dry, Jason got to know Joyce. Jason recognized that Dale and Joyce had an amazing relationship. Dale was devoted to his wife, very protective, always concerned about her needs and safety. They went everywhere together and seemed almost joined at the hip.

Jason decided to get to know both of them better. From an outward observation they seemed like an odd couple. The difference in height was the most obvious difference. Jason wondered that maybe by getting to know them better, he could come to understand how they managed to have such a long lasting loving relationship. Jason hung out at the counter next to the cash register when he was doing his laundry and talked to Joyce. He asked about her experience as an addiction recovery nurse.

Joyce had not started out working in addiction recovery. At first she was a cardiac care nurse. She became interested in addiction recovery when one of her children got addicted to pain

killers after being in an automobile accident. She learned what
she needed to help him get his life back together and found she
enjoyed helping people with addiction issues. She stayed in the
field for the rest of her career. Eventually Jason asked Joyce to tell
him the secret to a long marriage. Joyce laughed at the question.
Then she responded, "I think the secret to a long relationship is
knowing that there is something wrong with everybody"

"What do you mean, something wrong with everybody?" Jason
asked.

"There is something wrong with everyone. No matter who they
are, there is something wrong with everyone. Just put a random
number on it. Maybe seven things, maybe ten things." Joyce
responded.

"Okay." Jason said

"When I was young there were a lot of potential partners
around. I would go out to an event and there were a couple of
hundred people there. Half of them are the opposite sex. Out of
that fifty percent maybe twenty five percent would be a potential
date. If I went out with someone, and he would annoy me in
some way, I would just move on to another. It took me a while to
come to the understanding that there are things wrong with
everybody. I don't know if it was a product of getting older or
wiser or what, but it came to me that there is something wrong
with everybody. I was just trading these things that annoyed me
for other things that annoyed me." Joyce said.

Jason listened without responding. He waited and Joyce
continued.

"Compatibility is without a doubt as important as anything else
in a relationship. After that, it's learning to be accepting of the
things that are wrong with the person that you are with." Joyce
said.

"Wait a minute." Jason began. "There are some things that are
completely not okay. Abusive behavior for one thing.
Dishonesty, drug abuse, infidelity. Some things are not

acceptable."

"Yes, there are some character flaws that are not acceptable. But I'm not talking about those. I'm talking about all those little things that get on your nerves. The little habits or whatever that irritate you. That's what I'm talking about." Joyce said.

"Dale and I have a great relationship. To me a great relationship is two people who love each other and express that love by seeking to help their partner get what they want out of life. I want him to be happy and get what he wants and he wants me to be happy and get what I want."

"I see what you mean." Jason said.

As Jason was pondering what Joyce had said, a guest came up to the cash register and wanted to purchase a stuffed buffalo. Jason said goodbye to Joyce and returned to his laundry duties. Jason promised himself to think about what Joyce had said and looked back at his failed relationships to see if he was trading one set of annoying traits for another.

CHAPTER TWENTY-FIVE

The Lone Star Geyser

The days began to pass quicker. Jason, Stephanie and the rest of the group were getting into a rhythm. Everyone was getting out into the park and reporting their adventures to the rest of the crew. During the down times, between customers, everyone poured over trail guides, researching their next hike. The Circle of Fire Tour had given everyone an overview of the park. Now it was all about filling in the details.

Jason was constantly seeking someone to hike with. Unfortunately most of the married couples kept to themselves. If they wanted to partner up with someone, it was with another married couple. His available pool of hiking partners was limited to Stephanie, Jim, and Shelly. The schedule had everyone working half days and short hikes and general sightseeing filled the balance of these days. Everyone looked forward to their full days off to get in the longer hikes. Jason's Friday came around and he made plans with Stephanie.

The day started out with plans to go hiking on the De Lacey Creek trail that went down to Shoshone Lake. This trail is located on the road between the West Thumb and Old Faithful areas of the park and very near the continental divide. It was still early in the season and the beginning of the trail was mostly shaded from the sun. Snow covered approximately fifty percent of the trail and was between two and three feet thick. This was no problem for

Stephanie, she was light enough to walk on the frozen crust of the mounds she encountered every few feet. Jason on the other hand weighed more than twice Stephanie's weight and when he tried to walk down the trail he broke through the crust and stepped in a two foot hole. Not only did Jason step into a hole, but the snow in the hole would get up under his pants legs and was gathering and sticking to his socks and the inside of his pants. In no time at all Jason could feel his feet getting wet. This went on for a few hundred yards. He tried to walk around the mounds but getting off the trail was difficult due to the undergrowth. Finally he had to call a halt to the proceedings and refuse to go any further. They discussed the problem and Stephanie tried to talk him into continuing.

"I don't want to break my leg this early in the season. I simply cannot continue. This is going to be a miserable hike if I have to do this for the next couple of hours." Jason said.

Stephanie was not happy with his decision. At first when she showed so much disappointment at his refusal to continue, Jason was a little confused.

"I was really looking forward to this hike." Stephanie began. "My son and I went on a backpacking trip to this lake a few years ago and we had a great time. I was hoping to see the place again."

Jason put two and two together and figured out that she wanted to revisit a memory as much as take a hike.

"I'm sorry, I just can't do this. I promise as soon as the snow melts a little more I will do this hike. But right now, I can't."

She was a little put out by Jason's refusal to do the hike. Stephanie was in much better shape than Jason was and as they started to return to the trail head she started to pull ahead of him. She eventually got out of sight and ended up back at the car a full five minutes before he did. Anyone could tell that she was not happy about stopping the hike.

"Is there another hike nearby that we can do?" Jason asked as he walked up to the car.

Stephanie pulled out her trail book. After a little review she came up with the Lone Star Geyser Trail. She read the description to Jason and he was happy to hear that it was flat. The round trip distance was a little concerning but he didn't want to disappoint Stephanie again and he agreed to the hike.

The Lone Star Geyser is in a geyser basin southeast of the Old Faithful Inn. The geyser is located at the end of a two and a half mile trail. That made it a five mile round trip. The trail is actually what remains of a service road that followed the Firehole River back to the geyser. The road was mostly level and it was an easy walk. The area was not burned in the 1988 firestorm and the road is in the shade most of the day. The trail crosses the Firehole River over an old bridge and twists and turns along the river as it meanders its way along. The geyser only erupts every three hours or so. Stephanie had made and packed a lunch so the plan became to hike back to the geyser and have lunch hoping that they would be there at the right time to see the geyser erupt.

For Jason, the problem with the Lone Star Geyser trail was that it is flat and an easy walk. That meant that Jason had to talk along the way. Since Stephanie was a little out of sorts, Jason did most of the talking during the walk into the Geyser. He started with his early life when he lived in a small North Carolina town. It wasn't really small by North Carolina standards as it was the largest city in the state when Jason lived there.

"I grew up on the edge of civilization" Jason said.

"What?" Stephanie said.

"On the edge of civilization. I lived on a street with only seven houses before it ended, and then it was nothing but pine forest for as far as you could see." Jason answered.

"The place was a small town by most standards, only about a hundred thousand people." Jason continued

To Stephanie this was nowhere near the end of civilization. Stephanie lived in a small town but her father had a farm that was truly in the middle of nowhere. Stephanie however let Jason talk about the endless hours he spent roaming the woods and abandoned farms in the area. He went on to describe his childhood and growing up in the sixties. Stephanie listened and enjoyed the stories and slowly began to forgive him for stopping the De Lacy Trail hike.

The Lone Star Geyser trail was through pine forest and meadows and there were many opportunities to stop along the river and soak in the scenery. They sat for a while at the edge of the river and talked about the beauty of the area. Stephanie began to open up again and they began trading stories. It's funny how people do that. It is just a way of sharing and getting to know a person. Jason would tell the story of how one day he was walking home at night from the neighbor's house and as he crossed the back yard he stepped on a rake. The rake was laying in such a way that when he stepped on the end, the handle flew up and hit him in the face. Jason had a knot on his forehead for days after. Stephanie told him about the time when she was six and her father lowered her in a bucket into a cistern to clean it out. There was a log at the bottom of the cistern and they told her it was an alligator. As she got closer she got scared and fell out of the bucket into the cistern.

They were the type of stories that, when remembered, are laughed at but they weren't funny at the time. As they walked and talked the hours passed trading stories and memories, sharing their childhoods. Stephanie's memories centered on her father's farm. She lived on a mountain and the farm was about a thirty minute drive down the hill. Every day after school and on the weekends Stephanie was at the farm and every day there were chores to do. The farm was located in a long valley. It was a good size, with about a thousand acres that was roughly one half wooded and the rest divided into various pastures. Her father kept cows that were raised for beef. She helped make hay in the fields and stored it for winter feed. During the summer months, Stephanie and her brothers would stay in an old cabin on the farm.

83

Stephanie and Jason walked along for a while without talking. The road turned away from the river and was lined by tall pine trees on both sides. A meadow appeared on the right side of the road with grass about knee high. The meadow hooked to the left and disappeared around a stand of lodge pole pine trees two hundred yards from the road. The field was covered with wild flowers as far as the eye could see. The feel of the breeze and the sun on her face reminded Stephanie of the summer days on the farm when she was young. She decided to forgive Jason for bailing on the De Lacy Creek hike. She paused at the edge of the meadow and wondered at the thousands of flowers before her. An image of the Las Vegas desert flashed in her mind and she was struck by the contrast of the lush foliage before her and the sparse harshness of the desert.

"How did you end up in Vegas?" Stephanie asked.

"Just lucky I guess." Jason replied with a hint of a sarcasm.

Stephanie looked a little sideways at Jason. "Did you like living there?" There was a little impatience in her voice, so Jason decided to lose the sarcasm.

"I hated it. Jason replied.

"You would think with all the casinos and everything it would be an exciting place to live." Stephanie said.

Jason had learned a lot about Vegas during the few years that he had lived there. Las Vegas is a Spanish word for the Meadows. That was what Las Vegas once was, a meadow. At one time the valley was green when everything around it was brown. Artesian springs popped up in the middle of the valley from the snow packs on the surrounding mountains. Before the area was visited by non-native people, the water flowed through the valley making it green. Las Vegas is located in the Mojave Desert and it is in a valley with mountains on all sides.

The Mormons settled the place in 1854. The United States Army built a fort in 1864 and established what would be a long relationship between the Federal Government and the Las Vegas area. It then became a railroad stop and eventually a small town. It was a typical wild west town. Gold and minerals could be found in the surrounding hills and Las Vegas had a history of supplying the mines around southern Nevada. It got a little bigger when the Colorado River was dammed during the depression. Shortly thereafter gambling became an attraction. The funny thing is that most of the gambling is not even in Las Vegas. The Las Vegas Strip is located in the township of Paradise. But everyone thinks of it as Las Vegas. Now there are more than a million people who call Las Vegas home.

"It's a green spot in the middle of the desert with too many people and too little to do." Jason said.

"I would love to visit Vegas." Stephanie said.

"The town is a Mecca for tourist." Jason began. "It gets millions of visitors a year."

"It is a place of dreams. People fantasize about going to Las Vegas and hitting it rich at the gambling tables. It is a place where people let their hair down and go a little crazy." Stephanie said.

Jason did not respond immediately, he didn't want to come off too jaded or cynical, but the truth was that he was not a fan of Vegas. ""What happens in Las Vegas stays in Las Vegas" is an amazing advertising slogan that expresses the belief that it is okay to get outside of your comfort zone when in Vegas.

"That is a great slogan." Stephanie agreed.

"When you think of Vegas most people imagine the Las Vegas Strip. Where all the big hotels and casinos are."

"That's what I'm talking about. That's where I want to go."

"Yeah, well, the Eiffel Tower and the Statute of Liberty have small versions in Las Vegas. The hotels are built to look like famous destinations around the world. Why go to Venice, when you can go to a hotel in Vegas that looks like Venice and has canals with gondolas that you can ride around in, gazing up at a painted on sky as you float past shops on a street made up to look like Venice." Jason sarcasm had returned.

"It just seems like it's a good place to have a good time. All the restaurants, the shopping, sitting out by the pool all day drinking margaritas." Stephanie replied.

Jason had spent the previous few years in Lost Wages. Not Las Vegas. He called it Lost Wages for a number of reasons. To Jason, the place had no soul. It is a town that should not have ever been. It is in the middle of a desert. From Jason's point of view, Las Vegas is the armpit of America. It is brown, dirty and almost never rains and all the green is imported. From his point of view, if someone liked the austere barren lifeless look of the desert, then Las Vegas might be the place for them. Everything looks out of place. Building a house in a desert has got to be different than building one in a lush green local. When people came to Vegas, they built the houses that they knew back home. No one stopped to ask how the particular style of house might work in desert environment.

"I didn't live in the hotels on the strip. If you live in Vegas, it is a completely different experience." Jason said.

"How so?" Stephanie asked.

"The economy of Las Vegas is built upon gaming. Las Vegas has a hundred and fifty thousand hotel rooms with two beds to a room. That would be three hundred thousand beds. Hotels need people to clean the rooms and make the beds. You don't need a college education to make a bed. You don't even need a high school education. In fact, it may be a bad thing for a hotel worker to have an education. College educated people do live in the Vegas area, but the need is for worker bees to clean the hive and dutifully obey."

"Any entertainment that is independent or not associated with a casino is rare. If you want to go bowling, you have to go to a casino. If you want to go to the movies, ice skating, dancing, or just to get a drink, for the most part, you have to go to a casino. The casinos have a virtual monopoly so that if you want to have fun, it's in the casinos."

"Still it looks like a lot of fun" Stephanie said.

Jason could see how someone would think that this is okay. But there was a hidden threat for him. He could see all the lost souls that populated the casinos. The casinos were designed for only one purpose, to separate people from their money. Casinos have huge areas where anyone can play a game of chance and win or lose money. The great majority of the casino floor is occupied by slot machines. A slot machine is how casinos make most of their money. They are the most profitable game in the casino. The thing about a slot machine is that they are one person games. One person sitting alone at a slot machine pushing a button and watching a screen. Casinos are full of the sounds of slot machines. Bells and music going off all the time, filling the void that is a casino. What would it be like if every time someone pushed one of those buttons there was no noise? Imagine a huge room with people sitting at machines, putting money in and no noise? Jason had and it was depressing to him. It was lonely and sad to watch all those people living in front of a machine designed to take all of their money away.

"I guess I am a little jaded. To me, Las Vegas is a mirage in the desert, there is little that is real about it." Jason said.

Jason asked himself how he had ended up in Las Vegas. In many ways it was appropriate. The parallels to his life were easily drawn. When he first came to Vegas, he was burnt out. He had repeatedly lost at love. He had come to the conclusion that he did not possess the skill set for a successful relationship. Somewhere in the universe there was a line that he forgot to get in. The line where they passed out relationship skills. He had been married twice and divorced. Jason had a very long line of girlfriends that didn't work out. He had given up and had taken himself off the market. He was overweight and convinced himself that he liked being that way. Women left him alone when he was overweight. At least that is what he told himself. Of course eating was the only emotionally satisfying thing left in his life. So maybe the emotional satisfaction from eating was the reason he was heavy and not as a defense against the interest of the fairer sex.

Jason decided to change the topic and get the focus off Vegas. He walked along without saying anything.

It was sunny and clear and they were taking their time making their way back to the geyser. It took about two hours of walking and they arrived at the end of the trail. The scenery changed dramatically. The walk into the basin had been through lush wooded areas separated by grassy fields and wild flower covered meadows. The geyser basin was baron and desolate, the ground had little or no grass and the bare dirt was covered with a white chalky substance. Geysers and hot springs dissolve minerals far underground and the water carries the minerals to the surface. The geyser itself had a huge cone at its base created over time. For thousands of years, mineral laden water had shot up out of the ground and as the water left the geyser it immediately cooled, the minerals dissolved in the water returning to a solid state and forming a cone that grew taller and taller as the years passed. The cone was about fifteen feet tall. Water did not just come out of the geyser, there were springs all over the area. The spring waters were also laden with minerals that were deposited all along the surface paths of the spring water. This created the blanket of white crusty minerals that covered the area.

A small stand of trees with a couple of make shift benches stood about one hundred feet from the Lone Star Geyser. They decided that this was the best place possible to sit and eat. They made themselves comfortable and dug into the lunch. The stories continued while waiting for the geyser to erupt and eating. Stephanie was something of a health nut. She made turkey sandwiches and used twelve grain bread. Jason was a white bread kind of guy. To him the bread tasted a little like cardboard but he was hungry after the two and a half mile hike. He bit into the sandwich, he was surprised how good it tasted.

Stephanie and Jason had covered all the childhood memory kind of stories. It was time they moved on to more current events. Stephanie began by talking about her marriage.

"How long have you been married?" Jason began.

"I have been married for twenty-eight years. I had met my husband when I was eighteen and we began dating. We dated for seven years and then got married." She replied.

Stephanie said all this in a matter of fact manner. There was no twinkle in her eye when she talked about her marriage. She was distant and distracted, surveying the geyser basin. Jason had noticed that she was not wearing a wedding ring. She was after all in Yellowstone alone. When he first met Stephanie it was almost immediately apparent that there was friction in her life.

"Twenty eight years, that's amazing." Jason began. "I only made it to four years of marriage. How do you make it work?" He asked.

"I am not really sure that I have." She replied. "I have been married most of my life and I am not really sure I should be. There is so much between us. After all twenty-eight years is most of my life. To tell you the truth I am having a sort of mid-life crisis."

Stephanie wasn't looking at Jason when she said this. She was looking off in the distance. That wasn't really true either, she was looking off back in time. Remembering the past, thinking of the events that brought her to Yellowstone.

"What do you mean a midlife crisis?" Jason asked.

"I was miserable in Tennessee. I couldn't wait to be done. I had a financial planner and for the last ten years I have been working for the day that he told me that I had enough money to stop working. He told me that two years ago and I was ready to leave."

Stephanie continued to look off into the past. Her emotions didn't change. She was matter of fact and drone like, devoid of expression and emotionless. It was like she was reading from a script or reciting from memory. She wasn't present in Yellowstone sitting under a tree, waiting for a geyser to erupt. She was miles and years away, remembering.

89

"But isn't that something that makes you happy? You can retire and you have enough money so that you never have to work another day in your life." Jason asked.

Stephanie came back to the present and turned and looked at him. She really didn't know Jason that well and talking about her unhappiness with an acquaintance was out of character for her. She wanted to talk about it, but a life time of keeping up appearances was standing in her way. Preventing her from putting into words feelings that she had struggled with for years.

"I just had too much on my plate and I was a little overwhelmed. I had all this stress in my life and it was all bundled up in one big ball. The clinic and all the people that worked there all looked to me to solve all their problems. At the end I had two partners and I did all the work to run the business. I made all the decisions. My partners just wanted to show up and put in their time as vets. Any decisions about running the business fell on me. It was probably self-inflicted. I probably didn't let them help with the business and the way things were resulted. In retrospect I just could not give up the control."

Jason just sat and listened. He waited for Stephanie to continue. Jason was letting her find her limits to just how much she could say. She continued after a brief pause.

"And then there was my house. I love my house. We built it ourselves. I found the land and bought twenty-two wooded acres. We built the house after I had started the clinic. After building the house we started clearing the land. We built a pond and I made beds for flowers and plants. I had a garden where I grew all the vegetables we ate. It was great, but it turned into a lot of work. I didn't get any help from my family, it all fell on me."

Jason listened as Stephanie spoke. He was struck by the lack of emotion in her voice. She was reporting as if she was talking about someone else, someone she knew and not herself. Jason gave her a sympathetic nod of understanding and let her continue.

90

"Then there was my son. He is the center of my universe. I did everything with him. I went camping with him and his friends. I was the transportation and I got to go along. He was always at the house and so were his friends. I only had one child but it was like I had a whole pack of them. They would invade and stay for days. We had a pool and a large property with off road vehicle trails and a shooting range. It was a kid's paradise."

For the first time in this conversation Stephanie's eyes lit up and she smiled. She was clearly delighted remembering the time she spent with her son.

"But kids grow up; he graduated from high school and received an appointment to West Point. At eighteen he went off to school and suddenly I was basically alone. I went to his orientation and at the end of the presentation I was given two minutes to say goodbye. It was the hardest thing that I have ever had to do. I could not contact him for the first six weeks. It was a dramatic change in my life. It required me to make some adjustments. For the first time in almost twenty years I was alone in my home with my husband. It was just him and me."

This was the first time that Stephanie had mentioned her husband on this hike. She had spoken about him a little on the way up from Cody. Jason asked himself whether he really wanted to listen to a gripe session about that personal of a relationship. He decided to try and steer the conversation back to her son.

"An appointment to West Point, who did he have to kill to get that." Jason asked.

Stephanie looked at him and smiled.

"He was a great student. He was always at the top of his class. He joined Junior ROTC in high school and was the Captain of the Shooting Team. He was involved with a youth program that was called the Raiders. The Raiders were all about wilderness skills and outdoor living. From a very young age he knew he was headed for a career in the military. His grandfather on his father's side was an officer in the service. It had been a dream of his father's to join the service, but he did not have the grades to get into West Point. I think that is where it all came from. My son was living his father's dream."

"So did he get an appointment or did he get accepted on merit alone." Jason asked.

"He received a nomination." She began.

"A nomination, what is that?" Jason asked.

"There are a couple of ways of getting into West Point. Some people apply and are accepted on their academic accomplishments. Then there are the nominations. Each United States Senator and members of the House of Representatives has the privilege to nominate a person to be appointed to the Point. The Senators can nominate anyone who lives in their State and the Representatives can nominate anyone from their individual districts." She continued.

"He had the academic qualifications and had completed all of the prerequisites for admissions. He received the support of the head of the local Junior ROTC. I cannot tell you how proud we were of him. We were in attendance at his senior dinner and the school took the time to review the accomplishments of the graduating class. They listed the monetary value of all of the scholarships received by the graduating class. My son's appointment was by far the most costly scholarship received by any of the students."

As they sat there talking and eating their lunch, the geyser would occasionally spew out a little water. The geyser itself was not very visually interesting. It looked to Jason like a wart growing out of the ground. Each time that it would burp, they would pause in anticipation that this may be the main eruption. Since it only erupts every three and a half hours, luck was a factor in seeing the event. Visitors to the geyser record eruption times in a log near the makeshift benches. Jason had checked and they were there at the appropriate time to see an eruption. Finally the geyser burped and sputtered and began a flow of water that grew to a stream shooting into the sky that fanned out into a mist about thirty five feet above the top of the geyser. Although there were caution signs warning against approaching the geyser, Stephanie handed Jason her camera and instructed him to get her picture as she walked towards the geyser. The wind fanned the spray off to the right. Stephanie approached from the left, walking right up next to the base without getting wet. He got her picture and she returned to the lunch spot. The eruption lasted about twenty minutes and sputtered to an end. It was time to head back, so they packed up their stuff and began the return trip to the trail head.

CHAPTER TWENTY-SIX
Larmar Valley

The days were beginning to blend into each other with the inevitability that routine dictates. Short hikes on days when they were on the work schedule and expeditions on their off days. Jason continued to study the visitor's guides to Yellowstone. It was one of the ways he occupied his time while manning the cash register, waiting for customers. Eventually he began to read about wolves. Jason knew that Lynn was devoted to the wolves of Yellowstone and that she spent hours staked out wolf watching.

Lynn was on duty that day. Jason decided to walk down the aisle passed the reservation area to the Senior Guest Service Agents room. Jason wanted to talk about wolves and Lynn was always eager to share her love of wolves.

"I have been reading a little about the Wolves of Yellowstone." Jason began.

"You have." Lynn responded.

"I understand you like wolves." Jason continued.

"Yes, I do." Lynn said, looking up from her computer.

"Where is the best place to see a wolf?" Jason asked.

"The Lamar Valley." Replied Lynn.

From his reading, Jason had learned about Lamar Valley. It is river valley in the northeast corner of Yellowstone. The Lamar River is a tributary of the Yellowstone River and runs approximately forty miles through the length of the valley. This valley and its river are located entirely within Yellowstone National Park. The headwaters begin in the Absaroka Range, on the eastern edge of the park. The Lamar River then travels in a westerly direction until it joins with the Yellowstone River just below the Grand Canyon of the Yellowstone near Tower Junction.

The valley begins at the northeast entrance to Yellowstone at Cook City Montana and ends at Tower Junction near the center of the Park. The road through Lamar Valley runs down its middle and wildlife is easily viewable from a vehicle. Depending on the time of day, travelers can see bison, elk, deer, wolf, bear, osprey, bald eagles and otters. The valley has lush green grass that is framed by mountains and sky in the background. Bison can be spotted miles away standing out against the green back drop.

The Lamar Valley is remote, even by Yellowstone standards. A visitor to Yellowstone must go out of their way to visit the Valley. It is off the proverbial beaten path.

"What's the attraction?" Jason asked.

"I guess I just like the underdog. No pun intended." Lynn replied.

"What do you mean?" Jason said.

"In 1926 the last Wolf was killed in Yellowstone National Park." Lynn started. "The value of the wolf's presence in Yellowstone was not recognized back then. The wolf was a predator that killed livestock. The commercial interest of ranchers outweighed everything else in those days. So the wolf was hunted down and killed. Things changed and the interest of animals began to become important. As early as 1940, interest began in returning the wolf to Yellowstone. The endangered species act of 1973 eventually led to the return of wolves to Yellowstone in about 1995."

"Is that when you became interested in wolves?" Jason asked.

"I was interested in them before that. My husband and I were long haul truckers. We hit and killed a wolf while driving across

Wyoming. It broke my heart. It was a beautiful animal. Later, they started talking about returning the wolf to Yellowstone. I lived in Cody and all the ranchers were opposed to it. The papers were full of stories and I got on the side of the wolf." Lynn said.

"So why the Lamar Valley?" Jason asked.

"The Lamar Valley is the Serengeti of America. It is one of the best places to see wild life in North America. Since the reintroduction of wolves in Yellowstone, the Lamar Valley has been a preferred viewing spot." Lynn replied.

"Is that where you go?" Jason asked.

"That is where I first started watching wolves. The Druid pack of wolves that occupy the valley were made famous by PBS after being featured on the series Nature. On any given day, you can find wolf watchers with spotting scopes strategically located on valley high spots looking for wolves. We band together using radios to communicate with one another. Once wolf movement is spotted, the news travels out over the radios and references to landmarks around the valley are used to direct the watchers to the wolf activity. It's really a great place to watch Wolves." Lynn said.

"I am definitely putting the Lamar Valley on the must see list." Jason replied.

CHAPTER TWENTY-SEVEN

The Nurse's view

Stephanie learned that Joyce had a career as a registered nurse and had specialized in addiction recovery. She decided to make an effort to seek her advice.

"Someone told me that you were a nurse." Stephanie began.

"Yes, I spent forty five years as a nurse."

"What kind of nursing did you do?"

"I was a cardiac care nurse for the first twenty years. Then I switched to addiction recovery."

"Addiction recovery, how do you get into that?" Stephanie asked.

"It was my son. He got into a car accident and was seriously injured. He was in the hospital for a couple of weeks and on pain medication for many months. He got dependent on them and I helped him get off of them. That's when I got interested in the area and just started working on those wards." Joyce said.

"Have you ever heard of Compassion Fatigue?" Stephanie asked.

"Sure." Joyce responded. "It's something that happens to nurses all the time."

"I had a continuing education program about it and I am not sure what to think about it. I listened to the speaker talk about it and was certain that he was talking about me." Stephanie said.

"Well. I can tell you that in addiction recovery, it is a condition that effects nurses."

"I understand what it is, but how do you deal with it?" Stephanie asked.

"First recognizing that there maybe a problem is a giant step in dealing with it. The problem with busy professionals is that they don't have to time to take care of themselves. Joyce said.

I don't know what's causing me to feel dissatisfied. I have struggled with my feelings for a long time and this just came up recently.

"How long have you felt this way?" Joyce asked.

"For years." Stephanie paused, feelings welled up in her that she had trouble controlling. She was going to break down in the middle of the office in front of all of these people. "No" she said to herself. "Get yourself together." She took a breath and made herself smile. "I have been discontent for as long as I can remember. Ten years ago I wrote my husband a letter telling him that I wanted a divorce. I never gave him the letter, I just put away, hoping things would get better. "

"I wouldn't hang my hat on any one cause for your feelings. If you wanted a change in your life ten years ago, I doubt that it was a result of compassion fatigue, but I can't say for sure. I do know that time and space can give you a prospective that you would never have if you stayed in the middle of your life. Sometimes you just have to get away. Stepping away can give you a clarity that you can never achieve otherwise." Joyce said.

"Well, being here is certainly getting away from my life. I can't even make a phone call."

"It's also important to talk about your feelings. It can be quite a process of discovery, to simply talk about your feelings. It helps to see what is really brothering you and how you truly feel about things.

Stephanie felt relieved. She had not wanted to confront the possibility that her feelings about her life were caused by her job.

She loved being a veterinarian. She did not want to think that her feelings were the result of compassion fatigue.

"The truth is I should have left my husband years ago. After my son grew up and left the house, I just didn't want to be alone. I stayed because it was convenient." Stephanie said.

"Wasn't your husband supposed to come up with you?" Joyce asked.

"Yeah, he was set to come, but he bailed at the last minute. He said he wanted to stay and work some more. We had talked about retiring and he kept putting it off. After two years of making excuses I decided to start traveling without him. So here I am."

"If you ever need anyone to talk to, I would be happy to listen"

"Thanks, I may take you up on that."

Stephanie changed the subject and promised herself that she would think about it later. That night she went to bed early. She wrapped herself in her blankets and clutched an extra pillow against her chest. Shifting from side to side, she could not turn off the thoughts that assaulted her consciousness. She lingered in between, not really awake, but not asleep, trying to force herself to not to think, not to hear the questions that kept coming at her. It did not work, she had not found any answers, no peace, it would never end. Why did she think that leaving home would be an answer. It had all followed her here, there was no escaping it. And then it appeared. She tried not to let it in, but it would not be denied. She saw it in her minds eye, she was sitting on the bed and she injected herself in the calf and laid back on the bed and drifted away. No pain, just sleep. Tears welled up in her eyes, and she fought back. She thought about her son, she focused on him. The she forced the images out of her head and drifted off into a fitful sleep.

CHAPTER TWENTY-EIGHT

Elephant Back Mountain

The days were getting warmer and the blanket of cold covering Yellowstone was turning into a patchwork of white and brown. Hints of spring were beginning to appear around the edges of the melting snow.

The next work week passed without any major snafu's and everyone was talking about and planning what they would do on their days off. Jason asked for hiking partners without success. The most likely candidate, Mike and Hazel were making a quick trip home on their days off. Bob and Marna had plans with friend from a previous season in the park. Jim and Shelly were no where to be found and everyone else who hiked was working. The only person who was off and available to hike with was Stephanie.

Stephannie had lots of time to herself and spent much of it on solo hikes around the campground. She had a lot of thinking to do and was getting cabin fever sitting in her trailer on her off time. With nothing for distraction, it was hard not to stay caught up in her quest for clarity. She walked to tire herself out so she could sleep at night. It was the only way to quiet the committee in her head.

Jason asked and she was wanting to go hiking. The options for hiking were still limited. They decided to see if they could get up the trail to the top of Elephant Back Mountain.

At the north end of Lake Yellowstone is an area where the Lake

Hotel and the Lake lodge are located. Both of these structures have been in the park for many years. The area also includes a store and dorms for housing the seasonal employees that are needed to run the park. This small area of the park has a good population of both visitors and workers. Very near this area is Elephant Back Mountain and the access point for the trail to an overlook that showcases Lake Yellowstone and all the surrounding area.

The trail head for Elephant Back is a wide spot in the road just north of the turn off to the Lake Village area. The trail is marked by a small sign no more than two feet high. Off the road and up the trail a bit, a larger billboard type sign appears with information about the trail and a map of the terrain. The trail starts off walking straight into the woods and soon leads to the junction of two trails that complete a loop up and around to the lookout point. The walk around the loop and back is a shade less than four miles. The beginning of the walk is flat and easy. Jason was struck by the amount of fallen trees along the trail. Jason had heard about the fires of 1988 and the devastation that resulted. This area had not been touched by those fires.

Trees fall all the time in Yellowstone. The soil is loose and the tap root of the lodge pole pines is not very deep. This combination results in a lot of fallen trees. The effect on the forest was to make it appear is as if the floor was carpeted with a maze of fallen logs. For one reason or another, perhaps because of freezing temperatures, the logs all lose their bark. The climate does not promote decay and some of the logs have been on the ground for thirty or forty years. The park service does an excellent job of clearing the trees from the trail itself and as hikers walk the trail they are constantly passing places were a section of a fallen logs have been removed so that the trail is passable. In the beginning of the hike, it is hard to see more than two or three hundred feet in any direction. The trees completely surround the trail and block the view of the sky above. The trail winds through the trees, alternating between rises and falls in the landscape as it slowly begins to ascend the side of the mountain.

As they walked, Stephanie talked. Jason was still in a constant state of trying to catch his breath. This time Stephanie started to truly open up to him. Most people when they meet a new person, always wear their best clothes. Not literally, but people put on a front that represents themselves in a way that they would like to be seen. It's like dating. When they first start dating someone, they always wear their best clothes in the beginning. After a while they start to relax and become more confident in their relationship, they begin to wear the older more comfortable clothes. Its just human nature to want to be seen in the best light. Stephanie was opening up to Jason and for the most part he just listened.

She began talking about her possible midlife crisis. She started by saying that she had been struggling with her feelings for a long time and that she did not know why she could not see the answer.

"I have been thinking about this for a long time." She began. "I have this complicated life. I work at this clinic that employs thirty-five people that I originally started. I took on two partners but somehow I am still the manager of the business. I don't get paid any additional money to run the business but I shoulder all the responsibility. Do you have any idea what it is like to work in a place with thirty-five women under one roof, all cycling together?"

Jason didn't see a good way of answering this question. He decided not to directly answer and just encourage her to continue talking. "It must be interesting." Jason replied.

"I don't know if the clinic is really the problem." She continued. "I have been stressed at work but then again I don't get any support at home either. We have this beautiful house on twenty-two wooded acres on Signal Mountain in Tennessee. We bought the land and built a house. Over the years we improved the property. We put in a pool and built up the landscaping. We cleared the land and created a pond. The property is amazing and beautiful, but it all takes effort to maintain. All my husband wants to do is sit around and watch TV. "

"Sounds like most men I know." Jason said.

Jason listened as Stephanie recounted the story of her frustration. He was uncertain if she was just thinking out loud as a way of sorting through her feelings or if she really wanted to know his take on it all. He decided just to let her talk.

"This beautiful wonderful sanctuary has become such a burden to me because it all falls on me to take care of. I mow the grass, I clean the pool, I tend the garden beds, and I keep the place together. My husband is just a couch potato. "

"Then there's my son. He and I were more like friends than parent and child. He was an amazing child. He was always at the top of his class. He is charming and funny and we would go on adventures together camping, hiking and exploring the world. In many ways he was a surrogate husband for me. My husband always had an excuse why he could not go. So it was my son and his friends and me off to some adventure or another."

As Jason walked he was listening. Stephanie had talked about two areas of unhappiness. She was stressed at her work and her husband wasn't helping around the homestead. She also included her son while talking about her unhappiness and she had only said good things about him. He wondered why she had included him in the grouping. He decided to ask.

"It sounds like you have a wonderful relationship with your son" He said.

"Yes it was wonderful. But now he's grown up and no longer lives at home. He got an appointment to West Point and went away to college. He had been great fun and a good companion, but that all came to an end when he went away to school."

Stephanie stopped talking for a moment. She was time traveling, back to a place when her son was still young and a part of her life.

"He quit after his first two years at West Point. That was four years ago. Ever since then he has been drifting. He has started college twice since then and never completed anything. He has no direction." She remembered.

"Sometimes it takes a while to figure out what you want to do in life." Jason said.

"Yeah, but he will fall off the face of the earth for weeks at a time. I will call him and he will not call me back for weeks. He worked for a while for my father on the farm. My father had hoped that he would take over the farm and run it after his death. Then one day my son overheard my father saying that he was concerned about the fact that my son never finished anything. That was two years ago and they have not spoken since."

Jason continued listening. He was still having problems breathing. The trail had started to climb the side of the mountain. The trail came to a split which is where the loop began. The path to the right was a shorter distance to the top, but it was steeper. They decided to take the trail to the left which was the easier approach. Every now and then they would rest and wait for Jason's breathing to ease up. Still struggling for breath as he walked, he managed to ask Stephanie if she had discussed any of this with her husband.

"I have tried to talk to him about it. He just doesn't listen." Stephanie said.

"What does he say when you try and talk to him about it?" Jason asked.

"If I started talking about how I feel, he would tell me that I wasn't thinking right. I was just being emotional or he would tell me that I was mis-perceiving things. That it was all in my head. It made me distrust my own judgment. I was always second guessing myself trying to decide if what I felt was really true. He just always dismissed my concerns." Stephanie said

Jason listened as he struggled to walk up the trail. Whether Jason wanted to or not he was not capable of chiming in and offering any comment. Besides, a long time ago Jason had learned that sometimes people tell you things and they expect no

104

response at all. They are just putting a voice to a feeling, giving it air and hanging it in the universe. No response is necessary. The benefit is saying it out loud.

They continued up the trail and the level of conversation ebbed somewhat. Stephanie was having a little difficulty with the elevation of the hike. The route they took went to the left around the side of Elephant Back and eventually came around to approach the top from the rear. Just before reaching the top the landscape flattened out and they were able to pick up their pace a little. They eventually reached the top of Elephant Back.

The lookout spot on Elephant Back is a little in front of the top of the mountain. From this spot hikers can see the area known as the Lake area. The Lake Hotel stood facing south with a commanding view of Lake Yellowstone and beyond to the Grand Tetons. The employee dorms, a general store, a post office, a medical facility, and a ranger station are also in the area. The Lake Hotel is on the shore of Lake Yellowstone and has a great room with amazing views of the lake and the mountains that lay beyond. The view includes the entire plateau represented by Mount Washburn to the north, Lake Yellowstone and the mountains that reside to the east of the lake area, the West Thumb area, and the Mountains of the Grand Tetons to the South. It is truly a grand vista.

Jason had learned that Stephanie was a planner. She had packed them a lunch. In the lunch was a turkey sandwich, a sliced up apple, and several bite-size candy bars. Stephanie pulled her lunch bag out and offered him a sandwich. Jason did not know what it was about a sandwich and eating on the top of a mountain, but he truly had never enjoyed a turkey sandwich as much as he did sitting on the log overlooking Lake Yellowstone on the top of Elephant Back Mountain. It doesn't get any better than that. For whatever reason, maybe because there was still snow everywhere, they were completely alone on the top of elephant back. They had not seen a soul on their hike up and had the mountain to themselves. The majestic views before them were theirs and theirs alone.

The conversation turned to the landscape and the vistas that laid before them. They looked for places they recognized and tried to name the places they did not. Stephanie had brought a topographical map of the area and they were searching for the landmarks. Sitting at the lookout, the steam rising up from thermal features in the area could be seen above the trees and the surrounding terrain. In a vast expanse of trees running off into the distance, right in the middle, there would be a smoke like mist rising up from the ground. In no time at all, they had named all the tall mountains and identified all the thermal features they could see. Lake Yellowstone was surrounded by mountains on all sides. The air in the valley would gradually heat up as the sun beat down on the lake. The hot air was capped by a layer of colder air above, until finally the body of air over the lake would reach a low point in the surrounding mountains and pour out of the valley with colder air rushing in behind it. Jason and Stephanie watch as trees revealed the path of the wind flowing down the face of mountains side and spreading out over the water of the lake.

It was getting late so they packed up and headed back down the mountain. The walk down the mountain was just as hard as the walk up. The muscles in the legs that are used when walking down are different than the muscles that are used when walking up. Jason had as much trouble keeping his breath going down as he did going up. They eventually reached the truck and climbed back in for the short ride to the campground. Jason was exhausted when they got back. They stopped by the office to see what was going on. Marna, Jim and Shelly were working and standing around waiting for a customer to come in.

"Where're you been?" Marna asked as they walked in.

"Up Elephant Back" Stephanie said.

"Jason, are you limping?" Shelly asked.

"Stephanie is trying to kill me." Jason answered. "She keeps

dragging me up these mountains and she's trying to kill me."
Everyone smiled and looked at Stephanie.

"I went up it too." Stephanie protested.

"Yeah, but you're in decent shape. I'm a heart attack waiting to
happen." Jason replied.

"You'll live." Stephanie said. "You just need to keep hiking."

There were questions about the trail conditions and the views
from the top of the mountain. They gave a full account of the
afternoon and then said their goodbyes. Jason headed for his bus
and a nap.

Jason returned to the bus and settled in, thinking about all the
things that Stephanie had talked about on the hike. Relationships
were hard. Jason had had his fair share and managed to screw
them up. She had been married twenty eight years to the same
person. The best Jason was able to do was four. He had given
relationships a lot of consideration and had come to believe that
all relationships are a product of or result from negotiations. He
knew a little about what results when he did not know how to get
to an agreement. Maybe he could help Stephanie by talking about
his experiences.

CHAPTER TWENTY-NINE

Reflection on the Past

Stephanie sole and consuming purpose was understanding her life and the choices that she had made. In the morning, she would wake and lay in bed in her trailer, eyes closed and think for hours about her circumstances. She would travel back in time to when she was in school and dating her husband. She had first met him when she was eight-teen and with the exception of one short period when they broke up for six months, they dated until they got married eight years later. When they got married she felt that he was the best that she could do.

They had drifted apart over the years and had become more like roommates than married. Ten years ago, she had written him a letter explaining that she wanted a divorce. She had never delivered the letter and kept it in the nightstand next to her bed. She went through each of the reasons that she had listed for her unhappiness and compared them to how she felt now. She turned to what she had heard in the program about Compassion Fatigue that she had attended at the Vet Board meeting.

Reflecting back on Vet school, it did not take long before she was confronted with the fact that a large part of her responsibilities as a Veterinarian was to humanely euthanize pets. She was able to rationalize that most of the euthanasia was in the best interest of the pet. The dog lived a wonderful life in a loving home and it was suffering. The kind thing to do was to put the dog down and relieve it from its suffering.

Stephanie was community conscious and wanted to do her part by volunteering at the local animal shelter. Shelter work includes euthanizing the pets that were unwanted or not adoptable. As part of her responsibilities, she had to euthanize kittens. This required bottle feeding the kittens with formula laced with a drug to end their lives. Stephanie cried when she held the kittens in her arms and bottle fed them. It was more than she could take and she stopped volunteering at the shelter.

The problem was that there was a constant requirement to help end the life of a pet. In her practice, she had to perform two or three euthanasias at day. Over the course of twenty-eight years, this totaled a tremendous number of pets. She had discounted the possibility that she was suffering from Compassion Fatigue until she remember the neighbor and the puppies he drowned.

Her relationship with her husband, her son growing up and leaving, and the responsibilities of her practice were most likely causing her unhappiness. Going to Yellowstone was supposed to clear the deck. Here, she would have the time and space to think, to figure out what was causing her to feel the way she did.

Stephanie had difficulty of controlling the memories she was confronted with. Back in Tennessee she was busy, constantly working and interacting with people. Here, she did not have the defenses to the voice in her head. Whether she wanted to or not, she had to think. Stephanie kept herself as busy as she could. Everyday she would clean her trailer, whether it needed it or not. It did not help. The only time she could quite the voices, was when she was with Jason. She found herself thinking about him more and more. She allowed herself to imagine what it would be like to be with him. She wondered if he had ever done the same. The voices quited as she saw herself in a future where Jason was in her life. She clung to the thought and created a world where they were together and she was happy.

CHAPTER THIRTY

Pelican Point Hike

Pelican Point Hike was the next adventure on the "to be hiked" list. This is one of the shortest hikes in the Lake Yellowstone area. It is a one mile loop around the point. The point itself is covered with dense old growth coniferous woodlands contrasted by sandy beaches. To the east Pelican Creek empties into Lake Yellowstone. The mouth of the creek is either a marshy meadow or a meadow with a meandering stream depending on the time of year. The trail is flat and easy and can be completed in less than a half an hour. It is a great introduction to hiking in Yellowstone, especially if a person is not acclimated to the altitude. Stephanie and Jason had discussed the coming days off and it was decided that the hikes around the Lake were worth a look and if the weather would allow they should stack up several of the short hikes to knockout in a day.

The plan was a day of hiking and this hike was just the start. Shelly was on the hike. She and Jim had changed up their work schedule. Jim was deep in debt and wanted to work more hours so he picked up another day working as a campground attendant and now had only one day off.

Stephanie and Jason were never in a hurry on their hikes. They always wanted time to soak in the views. Jason liked to take pictures and videos and this takes up some time. They figured that it would take about an hour and then they could go over to the hike at Storm Point.

The trail head is located next to the road one mile east of the Fishing Bridge RV Park.

The junction for the loop trail was in the middle of a grassy field. They went clockwise around the loop. The trail continues from the junction towards the eastern side of the point. The grassy field gives way to small brush and pines. The trail follows the edge of the lake for a short distance then back off into the woods. Shelly led the way, with Stephanie following and Jason bringing up the rear.

It wasn't long before Stephanie's mothering instincts were starting to show. She was asking Shelly questions about her life and plans. It was a little like a job interview.

"Are you still in school?" She began. "Where do you see yourself in five years? Do you plan to start a family?" Living in a trailer park, there was just a matter of feet between the spaces. Jim and Shelly were parked next to Stephanie and she could hear every word that was said between them. It had gotten around the grapevine that they were arguing a lot.

"How"s Jim?" Stephanie asked.

"He's working a lot. He has a lot to cope with right now."

With everything that Jim had to deal with when he was a teenager, it is amazing that he came out sane. It did result in a pensive broodiness about Jim. His songs echoed the loss and despair that he surely felt during his teenage years. There was a seriousness about him. He pondered the deep connections in life and lectured Shelly. Life was frail and uncertain. Jim would explain how people were capable of connecting on deeper emotional levels. Shelly was empathetic and could experience at some level the heartache Jim recounted when he talked about his mother. She was the student and he was the professor, guiding her to a deeper understanding of life. The problem is that when a person is twenty three, they just want to have fun. Some of the glow was wearing off of Jim's story.

Stephanie never said it out loud, but she knew that there was trouble in paradise. Maybe Jim did need the money, but Shelly needed to come up for breath. The questions Stephanie asked were leading her to a place where Stephanie could bring up her relationship with Jim. It had come up somewhere along the way that Jim did not want to have children. It was hard for Stephanie to imagine a world where Shelly was childless. This was enough to raise red flags for Stephanie and a huge issue in her book.

Jason had been divorced a couple of times by the time he got to Yellowstone. He had two children and as far as he was concerned they were the best thing that ever happened to him. Jason also had found himself in his thirties and dating as a single father. He was dating other thirty somethings and noticed a profound difference in the women he dated. The difference seemed to relate to whether his date had children or not. He started paying attention and came to believe that having children changes a person. He knew that it had changed him dramatically. He had not decided whether it made them better or worse, he just believed that it changes them. He found that he personally preferred spending time with women who had children more than he did with women who had not. It was not scientific, but for Jason it was true. Jason listened with interest as Stephanie was talking to Shelly.

Stephanie recognized that Shelly would love to be a mother and that it was something that she should not deny herself. Stephanie wanted to help her see, to understand that Jim was not good long term material and that she should look hard at the future she would have with Jim.

Shelly was not in school. She had graduated from High School and became a hair stylist. She did not have any plans to go to college or to continue her education in anyway. Jason could see the disappointment in Stephanie's face. As they walked around the loop trail, Shelly told her story. She had met Jim at a night spot near her house. She had recently returned from moving to Boston and working at an upscale salon. She had spent a year in

112

Boston before returning home. Although she did not put it in words, she saw her trip to Boston as a failure and had returned home a bit broken. Her plans had been to make a name for herself in the big city. She had the gifts to be great at anything that she put her mind to. Her adventure turned into something other than she had envisioned. She had trouble making connections in the city. People were not the same as they were back home. They were not as friendly, as personal. When she met Jim, she was drifting.

Jim was in the band, the lead singer. She had gone to the nightspot as a diversion and met Jim when the band was on a break. He came up to her and introduced himself. It wasn't long before they were a couple. She was amazed by his talent as a musician. Music is the language of emotion and Shelly needed emotional sustenance. She was a little battered and abused by her recent adventure and someone paying attention to her made her feel better. Jim was expressive by nature and told her she was beautiful. This was music to Shelly's ears.

Jason listened while they talked and walked. Stephanie was confused about her own future and wondering about why she was unhappy. Sometimes it is easier for a person to see the faults in the decisions of others than it is to see the faults in their own decisions. Stephanie did not want Shelly to make the same mistake she had made. Stephanie's husband did not want children. Her son was an accident. He wanted her to terminate the pregnancy, but she refused. Her son was the best thing that had ever happened to her. Stephanie decided to share this with Shelly.

"I've told you about my son." Stephanie began.

"He's twenty five now, isn't he? Shelly ask.

"Yes, and he is the best thing that almost didn't happened to me." Stephanie said.

"What?" Shelly asked.

"My husband and I had argued about having children. I got

113

pregnant by accident. It was at a bad time for us. I had just quit my job and I was opening my own clinic. I had just bought a building and we were remodeling it. All of this was going on and I got pregnant." Stephanie said.

"Sounds like a bad time to have a baby." Shelly said.

"There is never really a good time to have a baby. It always makes changes in your life." Stephanie replied. "It did cause some problems. I opened the doors to my business when I was nine months pregnant. I was back to work two days after I had my son, but he is the best thing that ever happened to me."

Shelly listened as Stephanie finished her story. Shelly had grown up in a loving family with brothers and sisters and knew that what Stephanie was saying was true. She had nieces and nephews and loved spending time with them. Stephanie had planted the meme. Now it was time to let it alone and let Shelly imagine a life with children of her own.

The trail came to a place where the woods opened up and the view was revealed. Lake Yellowstone is a huge expanse of water, surrounded on all sides by mountains. In every direction there was one breathtaking view after another. Jason found a comfortable place to sit and Shelly and Stephanie followed suit. Everyone got out their cameras and talked about where to point and shoot. Another group of hikers came to the spot and it was time to leave them to their moment. The hike back to the trail head was through flat woodlands, only broken by the occasional wooden bridge over a gully or stream. It was back in the truck and off to the next hike.

Storm Point Trail Head is located further down the road to Cody about two miles east of the Fishing Bridge RV Park. The trail is a loop out to Storm Point and back. At the beginning of the trail is a small lake. This body of water is known as Indian Pond. There is a grassy field on the west side of the lake where the trail begins. The lake shore on the opposite side is covered with pine trees. Standing on the grassy shore, the trees on the opposite bank are reflected on the surface of the lake. The mirror image of the

114

trees is crowned by the mountains in the distance and capped off by the clear blue sky. The walk is flat and easy with a total distance of three and a third miles around the loop. A very short walk down the trail, hikers encounter the junction that completes the loop that is the Storm Point Trail and they can elect to go left or right to complete the loop.

They turned left or clockwise and came to the edge of Lake Yellowstone. At this point they were overlooking Mary Bay and across to Steamboat Point. Fallen logs and stumps provide ample places to sit along the edge of the bay. The trail continued southward along Mary Bay through a thickly wooded area then opening up to Storm Point. A colony of Marmots live in the rocky outcropping at Storm Point. They feed on the grasses that surround the outcropping and hikers delight in photographing the critters as they go about their daily activities. At Storm Point there is an upwelling of rocks something in the nature of the bow of a ship that sweeps up from the water line and stands proud before the waves ahead.

The first one to crawl up on the rocks was Shelly. She wanted to get her picture taken with Lake Yellowstone and the Grand Tetons as the backdrop. Stephanie and Jason in turn, had their pictures taken atop the rocks. The trail continues along the loop paralleling a sandy shore. Hikers can walk down to the water and along its edge. Stephanie called out when she spotted in the sand the paw prints of a bear that had recently made the same walk.

The meadow sloped down to the water's edge providing the perfect place to sit and soak in the rays of the sun and the surrounding landscape. Stephanie found a comfortable spot and Jason took a seat nearby. Shelly was standing just off to the right, closer to the water's edge.

"Ever think about going back to school?" Stephanie asked Shelly.

"College?" Shelly said turning away from Stephanie and staring off across Lake Yellowstone. "No, not really" She replied.

"No … Why not?" Stephanie said. "You're a smart girl. You can do whatever you decide you want to do."

"I never really saw myself going any further than high school and then becoming a beautician. What would I study? I have no idea how any of that works." Shelly replied.

"You don't have to know. You can find something that you are interested in after you're already there. That's what most people do." Stephanie said.

"I don't know what I'm going to do when I get back home. My sister needs someone to watch her kids when she is working. I'll do that for a while 'til I figure it out."

Stephanie refused to think about what a waste it would be for Shelly to babysit her life away. Stephanie had been in computer class with her and watched as she breezed through, picking up the material much easier than she did. Shelly was smart and Stephanie knew it. The group picked up and continued on the hike. Another short walk and the trail returns to a thickly wooded tree line. It was through the woods to the western edge of the meadow and on to the point where the trail joins making the loop complete.

CHAPTER THIRTY-ONE

Trip to Mammoth Hot Springs

Marna was the campground second in command but the leader in social activities. She was forever setting up gatherings of one sort or another. Most of the time it was cookouts for the staff that commemorated the passing holiday. She made every effort to ensure that everyone was included. She also liked to plan excursions to the local attractions around Yellowstone. Marna had decided that she would like to go visit the Mammoth Hot Springs and the Roosevelt Lodge area. Anyone was invited and it turned out that both Stephanie and Jason were off and interested in riding along. As it turned out Jim and Shelly were also available and piled into Marna's SUV for the trip to Mammoth Hot Springs.

Marna was married to Bob who was a worker bee at the campground. He was in the maintenance department and it was his job to clean the bathrooms throughout the campground and the shower facilities located at the main facility. He was also responsible for making site checks to ensure people who were supposed to leave did in fact leave and that anybody who was in the campground had properly checked in.

Traveling Yellowstone is different than in most other places. The campground crew came to call them bear jams. They could have been Buffalo jams or elk jams or coyote jams or any other number of other animals. Tourists were in the park to see the wildlife. When there was an animal near a major roadway, traffic came to a complete stop. Sometimes these jams would literally be five or six miles long. The road north from Fishing Bridge to Canyon traveled through the Hayden Valley. This Valley is one of the easiest places to view wildlife in Yellowstone National Park. The ever present Buffalo can almost always be seen from the roadway. Tourist season just so happens to collide or coincide with calving season for the Buffalo. Bears like to eat baby Buffalo. The combination of all these factors makes for frequent bear activity in the Hayden Valley. A pack of wolves also reside in the Valley and they prey on the Buffalo and elk in the area.

After traversing the first part of the trip from Fishing Bridge to Canyon they headeds over the Dunraven Pass to the Mammoth Hot Springs area. The Dunraven Pass is one of the highest in Yellowstone. The road continues passed Washburn Mountain and winds its way passed the Roosevelt Lodge and on to Mammoth Hot Springs.

During the trip there was a discussion about the various options and the decision was made to go have lunch in Gardiner Montana. Gardiner is a sleepy little town just outside the park borders. This little town played an important role in the history of Yellowstone. It is the home of the Roosevelt gate. When the park first opened all of the tourists came from this entrance to the park. This was back in the late 1800s and early 1900s when the best mode of travel was by train. A train that terminated in Gardner was the launching point for most visits into the park. Gardiner caters to outdoor adventurers. Whitewater rafting trip or a multi-day horse guided tour can be arranged from Gardner. A museum and historical research facility are located in there. Numerous restaurants cater to the travelers that come to visit Yellowstone. The plan was to find a cozy little restaurant along the Yellowstone River. The river runs right down the middle of town and restaurants with patios hang on the side of the hill overlooking the river. A nice restaurant was chosen and the group found an open table for six and settled in for lunch. Marna and Bob sat next to each other and so did Shelly and Jim. That left two seats next to each other for

Stephanie and Jason.

The restaurant had Western stamped all over it. It is a common motif all over Montana in restaurants and bars and almost everywhere else to hang animal heads from the walls. Deer, antelope, buffalo, and elk mounts were present in almost every eating establishment. In addition, horse tack, bridles, saddles and horse blankets all were used to flavor the establishment in the rustic Western theme. This restaurant included photos of the early explorers of Yellowstone and the rustic beginnings of the tourist trade in the area. Rusty metal pieces of the long ago past filled the void of the walls in between the animal mounts. Everything from farm and ranch implements to rusty old car parts. The floor was unfinished wooden planks with peanut shells strewn all over from the patrons constant munching of the buckets of peanuts located at every table in the establishment. The wait staff had an Eastern European accent. It seems that the local restaurants had to import help into the area to cover the business in the tourist season.

"How did you get to Yellowstone?" Stephanie asked Shelly

"It was really Jim's idea" Shelly said. She turned in Jim's direction and placed her hand on his arm. She smiled as she continued to explain. "We were living together in a motor home next to my parents' house. Jim needed a break from his music and we hoped that this might be an interesting adventure and way to spend the summer." Shelly answered.

Jason was watching both Jim and Shelly as Stephanie was asking her questions. Stephanie was the mothering type. He could tell that she had an interest in Shelly and was a little concerned about her life choices. Stephanie had spent some time with both Jim and Shelly on their prior hikes around Yellowstone. She had observed them interacting with one another.

"So, how did you two meet?" Marna asked.

"Jim was playing with a rock band at a local nightspot that I like to go to. He was the lead singer in the band and I got to know

119

him during the bands breaks." Shelly said while smiling shyly.

About this time the waitress shows up to take the order. It was chicken and burgers all around. The conversation continued trading stories back and forth about how everyone came to be in Yellowstone. Bob and Marna were returning for their third year. They lived just outside of Las Vegas and it was a miserable place to be during the summer. They made a habit of leaving the area for parts North and cooler temperatures. This is how they first came to be in Yellowstone. Stephanie explained her desire to travel and her recent retirement from her profession. Jason explained his wanderlust and the fact that in all his roaming, he had never been to this part of the country. Eventually lunch was delivered. The conversation continued with meaningless chatter that mostly centered on the campground and work.

After lunch the group walked up and down the streets of the town of Gardiner. Most of the shops catered to tourists and they were playing that role on this date. A short time later, they wrapped up their exploring and decided to head back into the park. In order to get back into the park they had to drive through the Roosevelt Gate, a large stone structure that was built in the early 1900s to commemorate Teddy Roosevelt's visit. Everyone wanted to stop and get their picture taken in front of the Gate. One by one all the pictures were taken and then everyone piled in and headed up to the Mammoth Hot Springs.

Mammoth Hot Springs is the northernmost hub in the Yellowstone National Park. It has year-round offices for the support personnel for the park. A post office and a courthouse are also located at Mammoth Hot Springs. The Army protected the park in its early days and they built a base at Mammoth. All that remains of the base today are houses. These houses were once the residence of the officers from the military post that was located at Mammoth Hot Springs. Today they are used by park employees.

The group took the opportunity to visit the area of the Hot Springs. An earthquake a number of years prior to their visit had interrupted the flow of water at the Hot Springs. Once there was a steady flow of water out the top of the side of a hill that cascaded down over multicolored mineral formations until the water reached a stream. All of these formations were now dry with the exception of one or two small areas. At best, all they could do was imagine what it would have been like had the water been present during their visit.

Elk like the Mammoth Hot Springs area. Open fields of mowed grass and numerous elk were scattered all about the area. The group spent about an hour walking around and exploring the Mammoth Hot Springs before deciding to move on to their next destination.

On the trip back from Mammoth Hot Springs there was a mama black bear and her cubs at the side of the road. The mama bear was foraging for food within fifty feet of the roadside and the tourist were stacked up alongside the road trying to get pictures of the bear. The baby bear had been deposited in a tree while its mother forged. This was a particularly difficult bear jam to get past. It took approximately an hour of creeping along the road before they managed to get free of the jam and head towards the Roosevelt Lodge.

The Grand Loop road takes you from the Mammoth Hot Springs to the Roosevelt Lodge. Along the way there is a stop off at Tower Falls. This is one of the most iconic attractions of Yellowstone National Park. It is a one hundred thirty-two foot waterfall on the Yellowstone River. It is called Tower Falls for large tower like rock formations. In order to get a good view of the falls you have to make a short hike to an observation point. The hike is downhill to the observation point and you can continue your hike down to the Yellowstone River. The group stopped to take in the waterfall and perhaps get some pictures. The walk down to the observation point was about twenty minutes. Everyone took turns taking each other's pictures with the falls in the background. The hike up the hill was a little tougher and approximately forty-five minutes later they arrived at the car and headed off to the Roosevelt Lodge.

The Roosevelt Lodge was constructed after the last visit of Teddy Roosevelt. Roosevelt liked the abundant wildlife and had a camping expedition in the area. A number of tourist attractions including a large horseback riding stable and a chuck wagon experience are located there. The chuck wagon experience involves taking a ride in a stagecoach a couple miles away from civilization to where there is an open pit barbecue. The tourist are fed a large steak dinner and entertained by a man playing the guitar and singing. It is one of the more popular activities in Yellowstone. The Roosevelt Lodge itself contains no place to sleep. The Lodge is a center or focal point for cabins that surround the Lodge itself. The Lodge is a log building with a porch out front. Inside in the great room is a restaurant that caters to tourists and the cabin occupants. After walking around Gardiner, exploring Mammoth Hot Springs and visiting Tower Falls it had been over four hours since lunch. The group decided to have dinner at the Roosevelt Lodge.

The day was taking on something of a strange quality. Although Stephanie and Jason were not a couple, they were basically hanging out together. Bob and Marna were married, Jim and Shelly were a couple, so that left Stephanie and Jason to sit together. They all joked, laughed, and talked all throughout dinner. It was all about the crazy guests, the complicated computer program, the crazy way the campground was run, and the peculiarities of all of the other campground workers. Finally after finishing the meal the group headed back to the campground. To Jason, it felt a little like family. He enjoyed Stephanie's company. In this group they were a de facto couple.

CHAPTER THIRTY-TWO

Shared Experiences

It was nine o'clock in the morning and Jason was seated behind the cash register when the doors opened. The morning rush consisted of morning shower people. It was a long wait for a shower in the evenings but in the morning a camper could usually walk right in and in about fifteen minutes the shower line was gone. Jason was left to sit and wait for something to happen.

Jason leaned back against the shelves behind him and put his feet on the edge of the shelves below the cash register. He was settling in to his usual relaxed state.

Mike and Hazel were working the reservation line. They too were busy just after the doors opened. The reservation lines disappeared and they stood behind their computer terminals and waited for something to do. The cash register was at one end of a long counter. The rest of the counter was occupied by guest service agents standing behind their computer. Today Mike was working on Jason's immediate left. Hazel was at the other end of the counter.

Jason and Mike bantered back and forth with meaningless drivel for a while. Jason described a recent hike that he had been on.

"I like that hike. I've done it a couple of times." Mike began.

"A couple of times? How'd you find time for that?" Jason asked.

"Hazel and I only live an hour's drive outside the park. We have been coming up here for years." Mike said.

"Oh, I remember. Jason said.

"How long have you two been married?" Jason asked.

"Forty three years, next June. Mike replied.

"That's amazing." Jason said. "Congratulations. What's the secret?"

Mike smiled and replied. "There's no secret. I'm just a saint."

"Really... She seems more the Saint than you do." Jason shot back.

"She is." Mike admitted.

So, what's the secret?" Jason asked again.

"I don't think there is a secret." Mike said. "But I can tell you that I think that constantly building a good past is as important as building a good future."

"What do you mean?" Jason asked.

"Working hard to secure your future and provide for your retirement is what most people focus on. I think that building a good past is just as important."

"Okay?" Jason said

"An experience like taking a hike becomes part of who a person is. Shared experiences builds bonds between people. If you take a trip and have an adventure, it becomes part of who you are. It helps shape and mold you. If you share that adventure with someone else, it builds bridges between you." Mike explained.

"Having a nice home is important too, isn't it?" Jason asked.

"You can buy a television and soon that television blends into the background of your life. Sure it is nice to be comfortable. But there are a lot of comfortable people who are miserable in their relationships." Mike said.

Jason ruminated on his own life and the relationships that he had been in. During his first marriage he went to school and worked and barely saw his wife for almost four years. After he got out of school, he had trouble agreeing on the things they would do in their spare time. During the entire course of their marriage, they had very few shared experiences.

Jason thought back to the conversation where Stephanie had talked about the fact that she and her husband had stopped having shared experiences years ago. Stephanie and her son would do things together, but her husband would not go. He just wanted to lounge around at home and go to work. It wasn't long before her husband started to blend into the background of her life.

Jason saw the wisdom in the things that Mike had said. He would have to think about this for a while. See if there was a pattern in his life and relationships.

CHAPTER THIRTY-THREE
Transition to relationship

Jason was spending a lot of time with Stephanie. Jason could see that she was struggling with making sense of the relationships in her life. Jason too had struggled with making sense of his relationships. Listening to Stephanie had caused Jason to reflect on his past and to revisit the mistakes that he had made.

Jason found himself analyzing the relationship and lives of the campground workers. Bob and Marna had a kind loving relationship and they were off exploring the world and living their lives to the fullest. They supported each other and it was clear that each one wanted the other to get full value out of their lives. They had what appeared to be a wonderful relationship. Lynn had been cheated out of her golden years. She had made due with collecting house guests and investing her time for the benefit of Yellowstone's wolves. Mike and Hazel had an amazing loving relationship after years of marriage. Shelly and Jim were just starting out as a couple. Trouble in paradise was certain to follow with them. Joyce and Dale were an odd couple that had an amazing relationship.

Jason was in one of the most beautiful places in the world. In this place, all he could do was think about what it takes to have a successful relationship. Jason went back to when he first got married. He really had no idea what he was doing, he was way too young. A baby was on the way and he loved her, he just did what he was supposed to do. They lived in an apartment in the back of her parent's garage. A grandmother's unit is what they used to call it. It's better than calling it a pregnant daughter's unit. Jason finished college and she was set to go. That was the deal. He would get his degree and then after he got a job, she would return to school and get hers. Jason started working and bringing in a good pay check and she started spending it. That was all there was to her returning to school. He didn't really mind at first because she took good care of him and their son. They had tried for another child, but it was not in the cards. Things were different after their son started school. She had no more excuses for staying at home and not finishing her education.

In retrospect the divorce was probably mostly his fault. When he was going to school, he didn't have time for much of anything else. He worked all day and went to school at night, leaving everything else to her. She made all the decisions about what they did as a couple. She was in charge of their social life. All Jason wanted to know is where he needed to be and what time he had to get there. She planned it all. Jason was focused on getting through school and getting his career going. Once he got out of school is when the problems started. Allowing her to make all of their plans as a couple set the stage for disagreement. Now he had leisure time and did not have someplace that he needed to be every minute of his waking life. Jason had put off a lot of things that he had always wanted to do and now he had the time to do them.

Problems arose when he started to bring up these things with his wife. She was resistant to any attempts to stretch his wings and fly on his own. She would plan a vacation to Yosemite, but he wanted to go to the Grand Canyon. They had been to Yosemite three times but had never been to the Grand Canyon. This was the simplest of examples. The dispute could have easily been about what to have for dinner. She was used to making all of the decisions and he never really cared. Now that he had the time to consider things, they would have disagreement about them. The

127

rub is what would happen when they disagreed. She would withhold affection. He was just like any other person on the planet and liked the physical closeness that comes with a relationship with a special someone. When they were not in agreement, she would become cold and distant. Jason did not like the withdrawal of physical contact. He wanted to be hugged, kissed and everything else. While they were arguing over something, all that went away. When he gave into her wishes, all that came back.

After a while Jason came to understand the relationship between their disagreements and the level of physical intimacy. When a person understands something it can take its power away. He started not giving in when they had a disagreement and not allowing the withdrawal of affection to affect him in the same way. This is where it all fell apart. The discord escalated to a point where they were fighting all of the time. He understood that her coldness was her way of getting what she wanted. He, however, did not have a way of coming to a different arrangement with her. He did not have the tools to work out another way of coming to a mutual decision about their way forward.

It all came to an end one day when they sat down at the kitchen table to talk things over. She started with a series of questions. When was she going to live in an expensive house up on the hill? She wanted an expensive car and she wanted to know when that was going to happen. She wanted him to go to work for a different firm, one that to her, was more prestigious. He sat there for a moment thinking about what she was saying. He did not necessarily want to live in the area she was thinking of and he did not care that much about the make of car that he drove. Jason liked the place that he worked and did not feel the need to change. So he told her, "I do not want to live up on the hill, I could care less about owning one of those cars and I am staying where I'm working, I like it there." She sat for a moment and looked at him. Then, she said, "I guess there is nothing in this relationship for me then." For a moment Jason sat there in silence. Without a word,

Jason got up from the table, walked out the door and never went back. It is hard to list everything that he lost when the relationship ended. The greatest loss of all was the time he could have spent with his son. He wanted to be a father to his son but ended up being a Disneyland dad, only seeing his son every other weekend.

Jason eventually came to understand that the relationship with his first wife did not have to end. If he was better at changing what had been the status quo to a new and different status they probably would still be married. He just did not know how to do it. He did not understand how to get what he wanted and keep what they had. When she looked at him as her ticket to a certain standard of living, he felt like he had been fooled from the start. It would explain how she could withdraw affection so easily. If nothing else it started him thinking about relationships as the product of negotiation. Society has created a template that people use as a frame work for a relationship. It's the details that need to be worked out. If he was ever to have a good and long lasting relationship, he had to learn how to reach agreement with that certain someone so that they both got what they want and needed out of the relationship.

CHAPTER THIRTY-FOUR
Mt Washburn

Mount Washburn is one of the highest peaks in Yellowstone at an elevation of ten thousand two hundred and forty two feet. At its summit is a fire lookout station with commanding views of the Mountains of Yellowstone. Mount Washburn is located north of Lake Yellowstone on the road between Canyon Village and Tower Junction. The trail to the top of Mount Washburn begins at Dunraven Pass, is a little over three miles long, and gains fourteen hundred feet in elevation along the way. Round trip is just less than six and a half miles. The trail follows an abandoned access road that switches back and forth as it climbs the mountain.

Climbing Mount Washburn had been the subject of conversation almost from the first moment Jason was in Yellowstone. It was a must do hike. Everyone wanted to complete the climb before the season was over. The comparison was made to Paris and the Eiffel tower. Not climbing Mount Washburn would be like going to Paris and not going to the Eiffel Tower.

The problem for Jason was that at the beginning of his stay in Yellowstone, he could not walk around the RV Park without getting out of breath. Climbing a mountain on a trail that began at eight thousand eight hundred feet and went to ten thousand two hundred feet seemed impossible.

Stephanie would regularly bring up the Mount Washburn hike

as a suggestion for their weekly adventures. Jason was very reluctant to agree to the hike. Mount Washburn was listed in the trail guide as a strenuous hike. The only other strenuous hike that he had completed was the Elephant Back Trail. Jason had found that to be very difficult and had to make numerous stops along the way. All this was before Stephanie hatched her plot to kill Jason. She had dragged him around on hike after hike for a few weeks. By this time they had hiked an average of three times per week and Jason was acclimated to the altitude and in much better shape. Reluctantly, he finally relented and agreed to attempt the hike.

The plan was to hike early in the day. This was done for a number of reasons not the least of which was that the trail was very popular and finding a place to park was harder later in the day. Avoiding the afternoon heat was also important as the trail guides described the hike as strenuous. This was the second abandoned road that Jason and Stephanie had the opportunity to hike. All of the other trails had been just that, trails. Walking on a road surface proved easier than walking on a rugged trail and Jason was having an easier time than he expected. Early on, at the end of the first switch back, the trail revealed its first hint of the amazing vistas in store for hikers. At this first overlook the view opened up to the south. The Grand Canyon of the Yellowstone and Hayden Valley are laid out in front. The view continued passed Lake Yellowstone, West Thumb and Flat Mountain. In the far distance, passed Mt Sheridan, the Grand Tetons drew the limit of where the eye could see. In such a place, the sheer majesty of Yellowstone could not be denied.

Stephanie and Jason fell into their usual routine. They would hike along and Jason would save his breath while Stephanie told him stories. Jason would ask the occasional question just to keep her stories coming. Stephanie was talking about Vet school. She had gone to college near her home but had to transfer to another city for a year to pick up prerequisites that were not offered by her local college. All during her undergraduate years, Stephanie worked for various animal hospitals and clinics. Vet school gave her a fund of knowledge and a frame work to understand the medical information she had to learn. It was the work in the clinics and hospitals that taught her how to be a vet.

"Education was stressed in my family. I was going to go to college and I was going to pay for it myself." Stephanie said.

"This was what was expected of me, it was compulsory. I started saving when I was very young. I worked at the farm and my mother gave me money for my time. I got a job in high school and saved the money. When I graduated from high school I had over ten thousand dollars in my bank account. "

During her college years she worked and paid her way along. The story was quite different for Jason.

"In my family no one ever spoke of college or even what I would do after I got out of high school." Jason said.

"But you went to College?" Stephanie said.

"Yeah, but I never once spoke with a student counselor about my future plans. When I was in high school, the Vietnam War was on display every night on the six o'clock news. There was no college deferment and I was certain that I would be belly up in a rice paddy six months after I got out of high school. I just got by in high school and barely graduated. I considered it was a waste of time thinking about college."

This was a totally different experience for Stephanie. There was a lag in the conversation for a moment and then she began.

"How did you find your way into college?" She asked.

"When I was a senior the Vietnam War began to wind down. The draft went to a lottery and my number did not get picked. I was a little lost as to what to do next. I had never spent much time thinking about what I would do after high school. I went to work for a loan company in a nine to five job and I lasted six months. I just couldn't see spending the rest of my life in that kind of a job. I decided to try and go to college."

"How did you get into college?" Stephanie asked.

"Where I lived anyone who graduated from high school could get into a junior college. That was the only requirement. I needed to get serious and get good grades so I went to junior college and got all A's. Then I transferred to a four year school, got my degree, and applied and was accepted at graduate school. All I had to do was work at a dead end job for six months to get the motivation to get an education."

Stephanie and Jason continued their climb. Jason was not requiring as many stops to catch his breath as he had been. Jason was able to talk more as they walked.

After about a mile they rose above the tree line and were offered views to the east which include the Absaroka Beartooth Wilderness. As they approach the second switch back, the fire tower at the summit of Mt Washburn comes into view. At first it appeared to be a squared off rock formation, but upon closer inspection its true nature was revealed. The mere speck of a fire tower caused Jason to question his ability to climb to the summit.

"We're going up there?" He began." Do you see how far away that is?"

Stephanie just looked at him and smiled. She knew that his protest was only momentary.

She waited without saying anything knowing that after a minute or two, Jason would back off his objection and continue the hike. She was right and they continued on. From this point the trail began to zig zag up the mountain. Eventually the trail comes to a point where it heads in a straight line that leads up to the summit. This section of the trail continues along the top of a ridge with steep drop offs just feet from either side of the trail. The sensation of walking across the top of the ridge was dizzying. It was only a few feet in either direction to a drop off of thousands of feet. The air was still on the morning they climbed the mountain. Jason imagined the effect a stiff wind could have on a hike as they crossed this section of the trail. They passed over this section and finally the trail met up with the Dunraven Spur Trail and circled around the last several hundred feet to the fire tower and summit.

The summit has been flattened into an area about fifty yards across. It is a circle with the fire tower on one side. A fence defines and protects the edge all along the circle. Hikers can get a three hundred and sixty degree view of Yellowstone from the summit. The fire tower has an indoor observation area with murals that identify all the features seen through the windows. This observation area has benches and they ate their lunch here as they absorbed the awesome vistas. In the back of this observation room there is a stairway that leads to a deck. The deck faces southeast and overlooks the Grand Canyon of the Yellowstone, Hayden Valley and the Grand Tetons. Hikers have their pictures taken with Yellowstone as a back drop. Stephanie and Jason took each other's photos just like all the other hikers.

As they were trading places for their photos a fellow hiker offered to take a picture of the both of them. There was a brief pause and Stephanie smiled, offered her camera and accepted the offer. They stood together next to the railing. Jason's arm was behind her and she had her shoulder next to his chest, hands clasped in front of her. They were standing there posed as a couple having their picture taken. They thanked the fellow hiker and Stephanie immediately went to her camera to review the photo. Examining the camera she smiled saying it was a good picture. Jason stood beside her and agreed that they did indeed look good.

The walk back down the mountain was uneventful, retracing their steps taking time to look out over Yellowstone. They returned to the truck and headed home having accomplished another goal and had seen Yellowstone from one of its most amazing vistas.

That night, back in his bus, Jason relaxed and began thinking about the day. He recalled the moment when they stood together having their picture taken at the summit. As they came closer for the picture at the summit, Jason felt energy surging through his body. It was like an electric charge building up the closer she

134

came.

Jason allowed himself to imagine that there was more between them. That they were a couple and that they were building the memories of their life together, exploring the world and seeking new adventures. He drifted off to sleep, clinging to the fantasy, dreaming of the possibilities.

CHAPTER THIRTY-FIVE

Relationships are a product of Negotiations

Stephanie and Jason were on another one of their supply trips to Cody. Eighty miles of winding canyon road where the safest speed you can ever go is about forty miles per hour, leads to a lot of long conversations. Stephanie had talked about her husband before. Jason listened wondering if something had come up or if she was just trying to see her future, but her relationship with her husband was on her mind.

"I am not happy with my husband and our relationship.": Stephanie began. "He is distant and unemotional. All he does all day is lay on the couch, watch TV and use the Internet."

"Sounds like most men I know." Jason said jokingly.

"Yeah, but we have basically led separate lives for the last ten years. We are really just roommates."

"Again, sounds like most married couples I know." Jason laughed.

"It's more than just that. I want to travel and see the world. We had planned our retirement and worked hard to get to the place where we had enough money to never work again. He was supposed to come up here with me and we were going to work here and explore the park. We both applied and at the last minute he canceled."

"Did he say why he wanted to cancel coming up here, did he give you a reason?" Jason asked.

136

Stephanie was a smart woman. She had been a professional and worked at her career for twenty eight years. She had been very successful in her career. A little skill at planning is required to succeed in any profession. Jason could see her planning her exit and golden years and working hard to make those plans a reality.

"At first he wanted to make enough money to buy himself a toy. He wanted a limited edition Ford Mustang. After he worked a year to make enough money to pay for one, he was going to retire. But after he got the Mustang, he wanted to make more money for a special college fund for our son. When we finally were ready to come up here, he got an opportunity to work a lot of overtime at his job. I don't have to tell you that we don't get paid anything here."

The frustration in Stephanie's voice was plain for anyone to hear. "That must be frustrating for you. To be all set to go and have him back out at the last minute." Jason said.

"Yes it was frustrating. It made me start to wonder about whether we would ever retire and start to travel. I am having trouble seeing a future where we go exploring and on adventures together."

"Have you confronted him about all this?" Jason asked.

"I have told him how I feel. But he tells me that it's all in my head. He says that my feelings are not real, that I mis-perceive the way things are or that I am just being overly emotional."

Jason listened as Stephanie spoke. Stephanie sat driving the truck, sort of collapsed onto herself. She was clearly affected by her husband's decision not to come to Yellowstone. It was as if she was feeling the burden of years of being denied her feelings. Years of being told how she should feel, what she should think. Jason felt confused and didn't understand this. She was a competent capable professional with an extensive education. Yet here she sat, dejected as if all her self-worth had been ripped from her soul.

"That doesn't seem right." He began. "You are entitled to your feelings. They are yours and no one should be able to tell you that you do not have those feelings. It sounds like to me that he is just dismissing your concerns without a good reason. He just doesn't want to address them and instead tells you that they don't exist."

"I don't know." Stephanie murmured." Maybe he's right. Maybe I am mis-perceiving or making up what I think is happening. Maybe I am being overly emotional."

"I don't know if you are or are not mis-perceiving anything." Jason answered. "Even if it is true, I don't think that it matters. You have a vision of what you want your future to be. Your vision includes your husband. If he has a different vision, then you should discuss that. You should discuss your future together."

"I believed that relationships require agreement." Jason continued. "He is not talking with you, he dismisses your wants, needs and concerns and simply tells you that you are imagining your feelings. From my point of view, it would not matter if you are mis-perceiving anything. All that matters is that's the way you feel and your feeling should be considered and discussed. You both should examine the relationship and determine how to deal with your feelings, not simply ignore them as imaginary."

'I can't get him to do that. He will not even listen to my concerns." Stephanie said.

"Well maybe you should just go on and live the life of retirement that you want, and let him sit and watch the TV." Jason responded.

"To be fair, I need to consider that I am not really feeling the way I think I am feeling. I don't know what is making me downhearted. It could be the clinic and all the problems that I have to deal with there, it could be the house and the maintenance that I have to do all the time. I am trying to sort it out in my mind. I keep asking myself what is making me so unhappy. It's like an onion or several lengths of string wound up in a ball. Everything is all mixed up together and intertwined and it's hard to determine just what the cause of my unhappiness is."

Jason waited a minute before he responded. Jason felt an attraction to Stephanie. He could easily develop feelings for Stephanie and did not want that fact affecting how he responded.

"That may be true, things may be intertwined and all that but still that doesn't give anyone the right to tell you that you don't feel the way you feel or to discount your opinions because they think that you are overly emotional or mis-perceiving things. You have the right to your feelings and that is all there is to that. The problem with letting someone do that to you is that you never even start a conversation. You never even get to begin. The person you are talking to shuts down everything by discounting your point of view completely to the point that there is nothing to talk about."

"If he will not discuss it then what can I do?" Stephanie asked

"You need to negotiate." I said.

"What do you mean negotiate?"

"I believe that all relationships are a product of negotiation. This starts even before the first date. Someone asked you out and says something like would you like to see the new movie that's coming out this weekend or something. They're making you an offer. The offer includes spending a little time with someone and seeing a movie that you may want to see. You say yes or no and so it begins."

"Yeah, but what does that have to do with me? I have been married for years." Stephanie asked.

"The negotiations never end. Most of the time the process is tempered by a genuine desire to do things that make other person happy. In other words, I truly want you to be happy and you truly want me to be happy so we talk and discuss and work things out so that we both get what we want in life. I may not want to go to the Grand Canyon for vacation. But it has always been your dream. I want you to be happy so the Grand Canyon is on the list of vacations we want to take. I have always wanted to go to

Alaska and that's not high on your list of wants to do. But you want me to be happy and Alaska is on the list too."

"But he will not even talk about any of this. Have you ever been in a relationship where someone wouldn't even agree to talk about things?"

"My first marriage ended because I didn't know how to negotiate.'

"What do you mean?"

"I got married before I completed my education. I graduated from college and went to graduate school. I worked while I was in graduate school and I had very long days. I was out of the house at nine in the morning and didn't return until about ten in the evening and that was Monday through Friday. I was very busy and focused. She was in charge of our free time. She would plan everything and I would just show up. If we went on vacation, she planned it. If we had dinner out with friends, she planned it. I didn' have time for anything other than my education and work. I let her take care of everything else. This all worked fine until I got out of school and got a job in my field. All of a sudden I had leisure time. It took me three years to get through graduate school and there was four years of college before that. For a long time I had put many things on the back burner." Jason explained.

"So what happened after you got out of school?"

"I wanted to do all the things that I had put on the back burner. I wanted a say in how we spent our leisure time. She had made all of those decisions for all that time and did not want to give up control."

"So why was that a problem? You couldn't just talk that out?"

" I didn't do a very good job of negotiating with her. We could have transitioned better and I could have gotten to do the things that I had put off for all those years. Instead, it led to disagreement and the conflict brought out other issues that eventually lead to us getting divorced."

140

"What other issues?" Stephanie asked.

"One of the things that happened when we had disagreements was that she withheld her affections."

"Everybody does that, its hard to cuddle when you're mad."

"It was more than that. She would not get her way and this would make her angry. She would not be affectionate to me in any way when she was mad at me. She would not kiss or hug me, let alone anything else. She would not talk to me, it went beyond her being unfriendly."

"How did you handle that?"

"I didn't like being treated like this so I would give in and let her get her way. Then she would turn on the affection. I saw a pattern and decided that I would not let this withdrawal of affection work any longer. I stood my ground and refused to give in to this ploy. It all came to a head when she wanted me to work for a certain large firm. We discussed the options and I would not relent. Other things were involved, but basically that was the end of our marriage."

"Where is the negotiation there?" Stephanie asked.

"That is really the point. There was no negotiation. I wanted something different. She wanted things to remain the same. We needed to work out a different agreement. Instead of finding a path to a new way of being together, we ended the marriage." Jason continued.

"I understand but again, he will not talk to me." Stephanie said.

"Not all negotiations are verbal. You can communicate in other ways. You coming up to Yellowstone without him is non-verbal communication. You are following a dream that you have had for years. By coming to Yellowstone without him, you are making a statement of how important it is to you." Jason said.

"But he refused to come with me." Stephanie replied.

"It does take two people to reach an agreement. If he is not interested in your wants and needs, then all the talk in the world,

141

verbal or otherwise is not going to get you to an agreement. Look around at the other people who work here. There are a lot of long term marriages among the crew here. Each of these couples has one thing in common. They all want their partner to get what they want out of life. They all want their partners to be happy. If you have that to start with, the agreeing part is easy. If you don't have that, then you'll never make any kind of agreement." Jason said.

"I'm afraid he doesn't care one way or the other about what I want. Stephanie replied.

Stephanie lamented on the years leading up to her coming to Yellowstone. She and her husband had lived separate lives. There were times when because of their work schedules, they did not seen each other for a week at a time. Stephanie remembered all the vacations she had taken where it was just her and her son. He stayed home, watched TV and worked overtime. She remembered how he claimed that her success came at the expense of his, how the distance between them had grown wider over the years.

"I don't see how we can ever agree on changing the way we live. We have grown in different directions. He wants a different life than I want. He values things more than people. I don't know if I can even trust him to be honest with me anymore. He signed up to come up here, but canceled at the last minute." Stephanie said.

The conversation fell silent. Jason was reflecting on his journey to reach Yellowstone and this place in time. How he had lost at love and his belief that sharing his life with a special someone was not in the cards. He wondered how hard Stephanie would try to resurrect the love that she once had with her husband. Jason would try if it was him. People are not disposable.

Stephanie felt defeated. She could see the obstacles in front of her. Her mind wandered through the years, counting the disappointments. The next thing she knew, she was turning into the access road to the campground. She dropped Jason off next to his bus and waited as he unloaded his groceries. After parking the truck, she entered her trailer and sat at the dinette. She could not remember when she had felt so alone.

CHAPTER THIRTY-SIX
Lake Lodge

Like almost everything else in Yellowstone, Lake Lodge is an old historic building. The Lake area is just a short distance down the road from Fishing Bridge. The Lodge is a rustic log building that features huge beams crossing large open areas. It is a meeting place more than a lodge. The front of the building welcomes visitors with a porch that stretched the entire length of the main room of the lodge. A center stair case leads up to the porch. Rocking chairs flank the stair case in both directions. Guest are welcome to laze away the day taking in the views from the porch. A cafeteria on the north end of the building is a welcome exception to the necessity of home cooked meals. On the south end of the building there is a gymnasium that is reserved exclusively for the use of the park employees. Nondescript cabins that populated the hill behind the lodge were the accommodations.

The long center portion of the Lodge is where campground workers spent some of their time. The long room is anchored at one end by a bar and a fireplace. Placed throughout the length of the room are conversation areas with overstuffed chairs and couches or dining tables. At the opposite end is a cluster of dining tables and couches that are spread out in front of a second large stone fireplace. This is where the campground crew would gather. Instead of eating at the RV park, everyone would prepare a dish and bring it to the tables at the Lodge. The food would be spread out to make a family-style dinner with other campground crew.

After the dinner was over the group would sometimes play cards or board games and entertain each other with stories from their varied backgrounds. Stephanie liked to talk about the employees at her clinic. She would often tell stories of how an employee found disaster in the simplest of tasks.

Jason had spent some considerable time learning the art of playing Texas hold 'em. Stephanie, Jim and Shelly had never played before. Jason was assigned the task of teaching everyone the basics of the game. On one of the Cody trips to Walmart, he picked up a poker set and was prepared to play instructor. After everyone had finished dinner, the table was cleared and the cards and chips were brought out. Without exception, the relative ranking of hands was completely unknown to them. Jason started with the basics and worked his way up to the more complicated rules of how betting was handled and how the cards were distributed during the course of the game. In no time at all, they were actually playing poker, betting, bluffing, and pushing the chips around the table. Poker night became a regular activity.

The trips to the Lake Lodge began to take on a special quality for Jason. He felt that he had missed out on having a family. He was divorced twice and had his children every other weekend. For Jason, there was something about a dinner table and sharing a meal. It is what families do every day, all over the world. It was a slice of life that Jason had longed for. Here, in Yellowstone, Jason was having dinner and enjoying the company of friends in a way that had not happened in a very long time.

CHAPTER THIRTY-SEVEN

Natural Bridge Hike

Just south of the Lake area is the Bridge Bay Marina. The marina is located in a small bay off of Lake Yellowstone with a campground just to the north of the Bay. A short distance behind the bay is a natural bridge. This feature is what the marina is named for. The hike begins at the Marina and leads back up to the natural bridge.

Stephanie parked the truck in the Bridge Bay Marina parking lot. The trail starts at the top of the parking lot and heads directly towards the Bridge Bay Campground. In about a hundred yards, at the edge of the campground, the trail turns to the left. The path continues around the bay passing through meadows and lightly wooded areas.

A short distance later it comes to a junction were the trail merges with an old access road. This old road is also known as the Howard Eton Trail. The park was set up to allow cars to drive right up to the various features and view them from the comfort of the car. Today, visitors have to walk to see most all of the various features in the park.

As was their usual custom, they talked as they walked.

"Jason, how many times have you been married." Stephanie asked out of the blue.

"Twice"

"How long did they last?"

"Just four year on both. "

"Who's idea was it to get divorced."

"First marriage, I wanted a divorce, the second I did not."

"I was standing in the church entry way, waiting for my father to walk me down the aisle." Stephanie began. "My father said to me "It's not too late. You don't have to get married." He had said that he did not think he was right for me. I didn't listen, I got married anyway."

"My friends said the same thing to me before I married my first wife. Even tried to kidnap me." Jason said. "You managed to stay married twenty five years. There had to be something there." Jason said.

"Yeah, but there were a lot of years when things were not good. We just shared an address for the last ten years. My son and I did everything together while my husband just sat at home on the Internet." Stephanie said.

Stephanie and Jason continued walking along. The old road came into a small valley with a creek running down the center. At places the creek is more like a bog and eventually disappeared completely. Following the valley the trail comes to a place where the creek entered the valley after cascading down the side of a cliff. The natural bridge is located at the top of the cascade. At first glance the natural bridge appeared more like a dark spot in the cliff.

"It's been hard unraveling all of this." Stephanie began. "I have agonized over this and I don't understand why I stayed with him all this time. I was too concerned about what everyone would think. We had what appeared from the outside to be a picture perfect marriage. We are successful, we have a nice house and an amazing child. I was maintaining an illusion. Now I understand. I was just pretending."

"Everybody does that." Jason said. "No one knows what goes on behind closed doors. You can fool yourself, thinking that you have no other options."

147

"I fooled myself thinking that after we retired, things would be better." Stephanie said.

They left the trail and walked up the creek about twenty yards and a light appeared through the hole in the cliff. The light was the sky behind the bridge. Stephanie consulted the trail guide and saw a trail that allowed hikers to walk behind the bridge. The trail climbs up the side of the cliff, loops around behind the natural bridge and then back down to the access road. The trail up to the right was a series of switch backs that led to the top of the ridge. A short distance down the ridge was the bridge. The creek had created a trough that lead to the hole in the side of the cliff. From behind it was easy to see through the space under the granite span that reached across the creek and created the bridge. Stephanie and Jason sat on the edge of the trough, peering through the back side of the bridge and took in the views of the lake, the harbor and all the surrounding forest.

"How can I go back?" She asked. "Now that I understand what I have been doing all this time. Pretending everything was all right. I can't un-ring that bell. I don't even know if he ever loved me. I feel like I was just a paycheck to him."

Jason was torn between what he wanted and what he knew was the right thing to do. He had kept his feelings to himself. He wanted to tell her that he could not stop thinking about her. How he laid awake at night and imagined what it would be like if there was more between them. The future that he imagined with her. Stephanie was at a crossroad. She had to make a decision about what her future would be. Jason believed that she should come to this decision on her own. In her own time. Jason chose the right thing.

"I have always believed that there are a lot of different kinds of intelligence." Jason said.

Stephanie was a little confused by the change of subject.

"What do you mean?" Stephanie asked.

"Some people are gifted at remembering facts and figures.

Others are good at math. Some people are good at more than one kind of intelligence and some are people are amazing at just one. I think that someone who is an artist is gifted with intelligence, just not one that we generally associate with success."

Stephanie laughed. "Neither one of those apply to me. It was hard for me to get through school."

"I think there is an academic intelligence that everyone recognizes and a social intelligence that is not as well identified. I have known people who in school were amazing students but were a complete failure at having a social life. Just as that was true, I have known people who had amazing social lives but barely passed in school. I don't have any idea how many kinds of intelligence there are but, I believe that there are a lot more than we talk about." Jason continued.

"For me it was training. I was very well trained when I got out of school. I really don't think that I am very smart."

Jason looked sideways at Stephanie. He knew that she was very smart and to Jason, it was one of Stephanie's most attractive qualities.

"You just never discovered the best approach to learning." Jason said.

"What do you mean? Stephanie asked

"I also think that people relate to the world differently. Some people are visual. The main way they interact and process information is through their sense of sight. This fact comes out in the way they verbalize their understanding. When something is explained to them, they will say "I see what you mean". Other people "hear what you are saying" and "I can feel for you". One is emotionally based and the other utilizes hearing as a primary method of relating to the world. Just as in intelligence, people can be very good at relating to the world through more than just one of the paths.

"How do you think I learn best?" Stephanie asked.

"I have no idea. You have to figure that out for yourself. I mentioned all of this for a reason. You have wondered whether you were ever in love with your husband and whether he was ever in love with you." Jason said.

"What does intelligence and relating to the word have to do with that?" Stephanie asked.

"Love is the same way. There are different ways that people express and understand love. What conveys love to me might not have that effect on someone else. You hear people talk about quality time with their loved ones. I believe that most men express their love through providing and caring for the ones they love. They are the bread winners, the handy man, and the protector. While they may express their love in this manner, they may perceive love differently. To the bread winner it may be acknowledgment and affirmation of their efforts that they understand as expression of love. It may be physical affection that reaches their heart. I just feel that understanding and feeling love comes in many different forms." Jason said.

Stephanie had listened to Jason and was reflecting back on her life. Her husband had grown resentful through the years. It all started when the company he worked at closed and he was offered a job in another state. Stephanie wanted to stay in her home town. She had just purchased a commercial property that she was converting to a clinic. He said she was not supporting his career. As it turned out the company that had offered him a job closed its doors within a year. This didn't change anything. The resentment remained and grew and the years passed.

"My husband did take care of things. If anything broke, I could always count on him taking care of it. I never had to worry about my car. Getting the oil changed or anything like that." Stephanie said.

"You said that you didn't know if your husband ever loved you." Jason began. "No one can really answer that question except you and your husband. One thing that I would do is think about how he treated you in your marriage. It's a statement or expression of his true feelings. Anyone can say they love you, that's easy. Treating you with respect and kindness is also saying I love you. We cherish the things we love. Protect them. Nurture them. Ask yourself, were you cherished, nurtured, protected and supported. Maybe you will find the answer to your question is not in what he said, but how he acted."

Jason suggested that they head back. They gathered up their things and returned to the truck. They talked about the campground and what another employee said or did. A light had come on and Stephanie had a clarity of thought that she had never experienced before. The question now was what to do next.

CHAPTER THIRTY-EIGHT

Husband no show

It had started out like any other day. Stephanie and Jason were going to Cody to stock up on supplies. They had traveled down the mountain and made their way to Walmart. As was their custom, they split up and did their shopping separately. They had arranged for a time to meet up to head back up the mountain. By the time they finished shopping it was getting dark. They stored their groceries in the back of the truck and left the parking lot to head back up the mountain.

The normal routine was to find a subject and start talking. Stephanie was fond of saying that she was having a mid-life crisis. Most of the time she couched the statement in humor. Today the subject she started talking about was her marriage. There was a serious tone to her voice.

"I spoke to my husband today" she began. "I asked him to take some of his vacation time and come up and stay with me for a while."

The cell phone coverage in Yellowstone was terrible, it was much better in Cody. Jason put together the fact that Stephanie had made some calls while she was shopping.

"When is he coming?" Jason asked.

"He's not." Stephanie responded with a slow exhaust of air from her lungs.

"What did he say when you asked him to come out. Jason

asked.

"He just made excuses. He has six weeks of saved up vacation and he can't take a couple of weeks and come and hang out with me in Yellowstone. He was supposed to come up here and work with me and he bailed out at the last minute. He wants to stay in town. The power plant is going to have a shut down and he can get a lot of overtime. It's all about the money."

Stephanie's eyes were fixed ahead as she guided the truck through twist and turns of the road to Fishing Bridge. The road followed a river as it ascended the mountains from the high flat plain that surrounded Cody. In places it was as if it hung in the air, following the contours of the hillside as it pushed out and drew back into the mountain.

A debate was raging in Stephanie's mind. What did it all mean, the years of living more like roommates than husband and wife? The distance that had developed between them. The resentment that had grown up over the year. Her husband was an engineer and had worked for an employer all of his life. Stephanie had taken another path. She had started her own practice and worked hard to make it grow and prosper. She was the true bread winner of the family, making more than twice her husband's income. He resented her for this. He blamed her for holding him back in his career. He had been laid off early in their marriage and had sought employment in another state. Stephanie refused to move away from her home town. Refused to close her practice and start again in another state. She had refused to place his career over her own. Her husband was unemployed for six months until he found the position at the power plant. He had been there almost twenty years now. But still he held on to the resentment that Stephanie would not sacrifice her career for his.

"Our financial planner had told us that we were done. That we had enough money to live the rest of our lives and never have to work again. That's why I sold my business. That's why we applied to work in Yellowstone for the summer. We have been talking about this for years."

153

Stephanie was quiet for a minute. Jason didn't know whether he should say anything or not.

"I was hoping that this trip would be the start of a new period in our marriage. That we would spend time together exploring and have adventures. That things would get better between us."

"Did you tell him that was what you were hoping this trip would be, a new start?" Jason asked.

"No, I wasn't sure that it could even be a new beginning. I wanted to come up here in a different environment and see how we did. I was hoping that being away from home and all the people and places we know, things may be different."

Stephanie had a reflective quality in her tone. She did not like the way she and her husband related to one another. How he dismissed her concerns and characterized her opinions as overly emotional. That he had said she would misperceive events and not get her facts right. Stephanie was questioning her take on reality. She was fighting the idea that what her husband was saying was indeed true. After all if a person is told something for long enough time, they can come to believe it.

Jason was conflicted. He liked Stephanie, and genuinely wanted to help her. At the same time he was glad that her husband was not coming up. It wasn't just that he and Stephanie spent most of their free time together and did not want to lose his activity partner. It was also that he was attracted to Stephanie and did not like the idea of Stephanie being with someone else. Jason pushed these feelings aside and tried to do the right thing.

"Sometimes, men define themselves by their jobs. The job gets rapped up into who they are. Men sometimes have trouble separating themselves from what they do. Is it possible that he is having trouble letting go of his job because he does not know how to be something different?" Jason asked.

"I don't know what to think. Maybe I am just a paycheck to him, his stuff is more important to him than I am. He has his fancy car and his tools. And then there are the guns. He loves guns and has hundreds of them. He kept delaying retirement so that he could buy a car and making overtime is very important to him."

"Maybe he doesn't want to do the same things that you want to do. Maybe he just wants to sit at home and watch TV. What then?" Jason asked.

"I don't want to be alone. I want someone to share my life with. To go exploring with. To do all the things that I have worked and planned for all my life."

Stephanie trailed off and watched the road as she drove up the mountain. Jason sat quietly thinking to himself. It was Jason's turn to look into the future. He had seen a future where he was traveling and adventuring around the country. In his vision he was alone. He had given up on the possibility of that "special someone" to share his life with. Three feet away was a kindred spirit. Someone who wanted the same things he did. Someone who envisioned a life that he had envisioned. Someone he could share his life with. Someone who was married to someone else. Jason refused to let himself think about the possibilities. Jason sat back and watched the road ahead. He followed the road's twists and turns as it climbed the mountain in the dark.

CHAPTER THIRTY-NINE
Meeting with Marna

Jason was on duty, waiting for his shift to end. He was eager to get back out exploring the park. As part of his end of shift procedures, he had to balance his drawer, make a deposit in the safe and lock up his bank. The lock box for the bank was in the campground manager's office. Jason walked into the office and said hello to Marna who was on duty and sitting at the manager's desk. He stowed his bank and turned to talk to Marna. She was not busy and he sat down for a chat. They talked about the shift that had just ended and the notable guests that had passed through registration. There came a lull in the conversation and out of the blue Marna said. "She's going to break your heart."

Jason sat for a moment, not responding, trying to decide if she was fishing or if she knew something that he didn't. The look on her face was genuine and concerned.

"Why do you say that?" He asked. He knew there was no sense pretending. He had always worn his feeling on his sleeve. Anyone who bothered to pay attention would have seen how he felt. And then there was the fact that he and Stephanie spent most of their off time together. You didn't have to be Sherlock Holmes to add two and two together.

"I just know. She is going to break your heart. She has a lot on her plate and she does not know where to start. You're going to get hurt, if you're not careful."

156

"I" Jason caught himself, chocking the argument he was about to offer, He knew she was concerned and not just engaging in idle gossip.

"I - - Jason stopped again as Marna continued.

"It is obvious that you have feelings for her. Have you told her?"

"No, I can't do that.

Jason sat for a moment, thinking about what had just been brought out into the light. He wasn't ready to confront his feelings. He had come to the conclusion that Stephanie was escaping, She had reached her maximum capacity and was shedding stressful relationships in her life. She was declining, unable to cope, to deal with stress and anxiety. She was going down into an abyss.

"You're probably right." He finally admitted. "But sometimes you have no choice, you have to see where thing go. "

Jason paused shifting in his chair. Unable to find a comfortable position.

"If I told her, it would make things worse. I struggle with doing the right thing and doing what I want. It would be a rebound relationship and that's a bad way to start. I also don't want to influence her decision about her marriage. She tells me that it has not been good for a long time, but she has done nothing to make it better or end it.   The problem that I am having is that on a rational basis I know what I should do, but for emotional reasons, I can't. I've been thinking about leaving, ending the season early and going down the road." Jason voice betrayed a lack of conviction. He would never go and he knew it. He had a tiger by the tail and he was going to hold on at all cost.

Marna looked across the desk at Jason and could see the conflict in his eyes. She knew that there was nothing she could say that would alter Jason course.

"I understand, but just be careful" She said. Jason nodded his head in recognition of the truth in her statement   He sat for a moment in silence. "Will see what we will see." Jason said in a hushed tone and left the office.

CHAPTER FORTY

text message

Stephanie's RV was a fifth wheel trailer. The bedroom was upstairs in the part of the trailer that was connected to the truck. The back of the trailer had a kitchen and living room area. A couple of reclining chairs and a dinette completed the appointments. Jason was relaxing in a reclining chair reading a trail guide as Stephanie was preparing food. They had planned an afternoon hike and were waiting for the weather to break. It was late July and snowing outside. The snow was not sticking, but still it was snowing outside. They had decided to have lunch and see how the weather turned.

Stephanie's phone signaled a text message and she reached for it, pushing the read button. Stephanie stared at the screen for just a second. As she read the text her eyes teared up and she began to flush. She threw the phone on the dinette bench and quickly turned, walking up the stairs to the bathroom.

Jason was surprised by Stephanie's emotional response and wondered what it could be all about. Without thinking he reached for the phone and looked at the text. It was from Stephanie's husband. Jason knew that Stephanie had tried to get him to come up to Yellowstone for a couple of weeks. He did not read the text.

Jason quickly returned the phone to its position on the bench. He was puzzled by Stephanie's emotional response to the

159

message. Stephanie lingered in the bathroom. When she came out, she returned to preparing lunch without making eye contact with Jason.

"Everything okay? Jason asked.

Stephanie didn't respond immediately. She focused on the food she was preparing, making tea and clearing up the counter. "Yes." She finally said.

"You seemed upset by the phone message." Jason said.

"It was my husband. We had been talking about him coming to visit. It's frustrating." Stephanie said.

"Is he coming up?" Jason asked.

Stephanie did not respond immediately. She was still at the counter with her back to Jason. "We're still talking about it."

Jason listened to Stephanie's response. He knew there was more. He felt angry when he saw the distress in her face when she read the message. He wondered what could cause such a reaction.

Jason decided to push it all out of his mind, refused to think about it. They enjoyed their lunch together, talking about nothing and watching the weather out the window. The time raced by as the talked and laughed, enjoying each other's company. It became obvious that the weather was not going to cooperate and they decided to call it a day. They made plans to try again the next day and Jason returned to his bus.

CHAPTER FORTY-ONE

I can change him

The following day Stephanie and Jason got together in the morning to go on the sewer road. This was a walk they would do when they only had a couple of hours available to go hiking. The road was behind the Fishing Bridge area and led back to a waste water treatment plant. They just called it the sewer road. Stephanie had gotten to the point where most of her waking moments were devoted to trying to understanding her life. Most of her conversations were surrounding her situation with either the clinic, her marriage, or her son. On this particular occasion, she was talking about her husband.

"I can change him." She said. "He just needs to get up out of the chair and stop watching TV. I want to go exploring and travel. We had talked about it for years. We had finally gotten to the point where we could retire and he is dragging his feet."

Jason did not respond to her statement. He flashed back to his life and the relationships that he had been in. Jason was not a stranger to the "I can change him" philosophy. He had on many occasions been the target of an "I can change him" campaign. He remembered back to his first marriage and the desire by his wife that she live in a certain area, drive a certain car and that he work for a certain employer. That was one of the first of many attempts to get him to change. More often it was much more subtle. His significant other would buy him a certain style of clothes, prepare a vegetarian meal or get tickets to the opera. When Jason was not working, he wore blue jeans. He was a meat eater and only listened to classic rock and country. That did not mean that Jason could not change his ways. But from his experience the changes in his life were made after reflection on how someone else did something and not because someone had mounted an "I can change him campaign."

"You can't change him, especially if he has no interest in changing." Jason began. "You can only change yourself. You can only control what you do and how you act. All that you can hope for is that he sees the changes in you and reflects them back to you. If he is indeed capable of changing and willing."

Stephanie listened as Jason spoke, but she was not convinced. Stephanie was tenacious and determined. But there was something else going on behind the scenes. Jason had seen Stephanie on the phone with her husband on several occasions. There was a change in her mannerisms and demeanor during these phone calls. She seemed to shut down and change her posture, folding into herself. It was like she was cowering. This body language was not consistent with the person that Jason had come to know. Stephanie was a capable hard driven businesswoman who had a career of accomplishments that anyone would be proud of. However when she spoke to her husband, her body language and demeanor screamed that she was frightened of her husband for some reason.

There was a frustration in Stephanie's voice. She had a history of getting what she went after. Jason listened as she spoke, but decided that he had said enough. They walked to the sewer plant and returned to the campground.

CHAPTER FORTY-TWO
Bunsen Peak Trail

The Gallitan Range is located in the northwest corner of Yellowstone. The tallest peak in the range is Electric Peak which is over ten thousand feet high. The range leaves the northwest corner of Wyoming and travels through much of Montana. The Yellowstone River flows along its slopes. Bunsen Peak is due south of the Mammoth Hot Springs area. Following the road from Mammoth Hot Springs to the Norris area it will go through Kingman Pass and the peak is on the east side of the pass. The peak's first name of Observation Mountain did not stick and it was eventually renamed after a famous German chemist Robert Bunsen, the inventor of the Bunsen Burner. The inventor was famous not only for the laboratory device but also for the fact that he had developed early theories about volcanic geysers.

Jason had been making excuses and avoiding this hike for some time. Stephanie had it on her bucket list and would not be denied. Jason was now fine on flat and long hikes and had gotten better with the change in altitude. Hiking uphill still robbed him of his wind and Bunsen Peak was a climb. He was in better shape now and Stephanie knew it, there were no more excuses.

Stephanie and Jason left the RV Park early. The temperature only got up to around seventy degrees at this time of year in Yellowstone. This was not the problem. It was going to be a clear day and with the sun and the exertion required to climb the peak, they were worried about getting overheated. As they drove they made small talk. This was an area of the park where they had not spent much time. They drove north on the Loop Road towards the Canyon area. At Canyon they turned left to head in the direction of Norris. It was a right turn at the Norris Junction. The road between Norris and Mammoth was under construction. The park Service was widening the road and it had been scheduled to close early for the year. This was one of the reasons that Stephanie wanted to get to this hike. Due to the pending road closure, if they did not get to the hike now, they would not be able to do the hike at all.

The area was badly burned in the 1988 fire that devastated Yellowstone. Bunsen peak is an ancient volcano cone. It's not often that a person gets the chance to climb to the top of a volcano. When they got to the trail head, they discovered a notice on the trail head sign that the trail was closed due to bear activity. This most likely meant one of two things. Bears are protective of food. If a hiker stumbled upon a bear on a carcass, they could be in trouble. The rangers will close a trail if there are feeding bears in the area. Another reason for closing the trail is that there was a close encounter with a bear. The notice was dated the day before. Stephanie was convinced that the closure was for the date shown on the notice only. Jason argued with her that it was closed until the notice was removed but Stephanie would not be denied and they were soon hiking up the trail.

The hike from the trail head to the summit is a steep two miles that ascends about thirteen hundred feet. The beginning of the trail goes through a thicket of new pine trees. This was the area that was burned out in the 1988 firestorm. It was hard to see much of anything other than the trail itself. After a relatively short walk, the trail comes to a pine forest that is more open and with older growth.

Every living thing requires the right conditions to exist. There is a limit as to how high up in altitude a tree can grow. This

altitude can be seen on mountain sides and is called the tree-line.
As the altitude increases and nears this line, the trees will not
grow normally. They are stunted and appear twisted or wind
swept. Most of Yellowstone is just below the tree-line. The forest
that embraces the tree line are call sub-alpine and most of
Yellowstone is a sub-alpine forest.

The overwhelming majority of the trees in the forested areas of
the park are lodgepole pine. The tree takes its name from the trees
used as the framework for the Native American tepee. The
lodgepole is dependent upon fire for reproduction. The cones
require the heat of the fire to open up and spread its seeds. In
some parts of the park, the forest floor is carpeted with fallen
trees. The combination of the loose soil, shallow roots, and strong
winds caused the trees to fall. In the high altitude of Yellowstone
trees do not rot quickly. A tree that fell thirty years ago could
appear like it fell yesterday.

In short order the trail clears the tree line completely and
ascends the slopes in open country. The views are panoramic.
Hikers can see across a large valley just south of Bunsen Peak.
The road from Norris runs through the valley and is sprinkled
with small lakes and streams. This road follows a stream as it
makes its way through the pass headed north towards Mammoth
Hot Springs. A short walk across the side of the base of the
mountain and the trail come to the beginning of the switch backs.
At this point hikers can see Mammoth Hot Springs. Jason got his
camera out and set up the tripod to get some footage. He zoomed
in on the hot springs and slowly pulled back revealing the
distance and grandness of the view. Turning onto the first switch
back they were again facing south towards Norris. Shortly
thereafter they encountered loose rocks that the trail must
traverse, but for the most part the walk was on solid footing.
After a series of switch backs they arrived at another very rocky
area just below the peak. Finally they reached the top and
discovered a small wooden building that was connected to
various antennas and had a sign on the door that said

"communication equipment". A little further on there is the remains of a foundation that they considered a possible place to eat their packed lunch.

They moved passed the remains of the foundation and followed the crest line for a few hundred yards. It quickly became obvious that the best place to stop was the foundation site, so they returned and settled in for a meal. Stephanie was a planner. She also took very good care of Jason on these hikes. She had packed a turkey sandwich with sliced fruit and dessert. They settled in, propping themselves up against the slanted sides of foundation blocks. The views of the surrounding terrain were completely unobstructed. They were on the top of the world. Stephanie opened her pack and pulled out the bag containing lunch. "I don't know what it is, but food just tastes better on top of a mountain." Jason said. Stephanie handed him his meal and he attacked his sandwich first.

Stephanie has well ingrained mothering instincts. It was a turkey sandwich on whole wheat bread with romaine leaves and hot house grown tomatoes. Jason wasn't about to complain.

"When I was younger I lived in the south and we had a saying. It went something like "I wonder what the poor people are doing?" We were not rich by any means. Whenever we would do something special this phrase would be repeated. By special it could be as simple as having ice cream on a hot summer night. "So, I wonder what the poor people are doing?"" Jason stated.

Stephanie just looked at him and smiled. She was eating her sandwich and just taking in the experience of sitting on top of a volcano in the middle of Yellowstone. About that time a squirrel presented himself on a nearby rock. He was a fat little fellow and appeared to have little concern about whether he was on the menu or not. He was concerned about what Stephanie and Jason were eating. He came right over to where they were sitting and jumped up on Jason's out stretched legs.

"That is cute stuff." Stephanie commented as the squirrel looked around.

It wasn't long before the squirrel had assessed the situation and planned his next move. He turned towards a bag of sun chips that Jason had placed near his feet in between Stephanie and himself . As he made tentative steps toward the bag of chips Jason tried to warn him away with a "no, no, no." He remained undaunted. Of course in reply to Jason's no, no, no, Stephanie is saying "yes, yes, yes." Jason protested that they were his sun chips and he couldn't have any. The squirrel climbed down off Jason's shin and circled around the bag searching for the opening. Once he found the spot, he dove in so that the only thing visible was his tail and rear end sticking out of the bag. In an instant, he popped his head out with sun chips in his mouth and dashed away with his prize.

Jason and Stephanie laughed at the antics of the little squirrel. As soon as he had disappeared, he returned. The squirrel had munched up the sun chip and stored it in his cheek pouches. He returned to his perch on Jason's leg, surveying his next foray into their food supply. Just before his return, Stephanie had taken out a mini peanut butter cup from her supply of goodies. The bandit paused to consider his next move. He passed by the bag of chips and crossed the divide between Jason's legs and the outstretched legs of Stephanie. He lingered for a moment, then jumped onto Stephanie's shin. Slowly, he began moving up her leg, stopping every few steps to appraise the potential for danger. Stephanie was holding the peanut butter cup in her hands which were resting in her lap. The bandit slowly approached and with his front paws, opened Stephanie's hand, reached in and grabbed the peanut butter cup with his teeth. Once securely latched on, he darted off behind a rock with his prize.

Jason and Stephanie fell over they were laughing so hard. It was a moment in time shared just between the two of them. Jason remembered the advice he had received from Mike about building memories in a relationship. Jason was building shared memories with Stephanie. Jason had not allowed himself to think about Stephanie as anything other than a friend. But things had changed since he first met Stephanie. She had confided in him about her unhappy life. Stephanie was with him on the top of a mountain in one of the most beautiful places in the world. Maybe it was time to start thinking about possibilities.

CHAPTER FORTY-THREE

Connections

"Did you hear about Jim and Shelly" Jason asked.

"Hear what." Stephanie replied. "I live right next to them and I hear them all the time, yelling at each other."

"They're leaving early. Pulling out tomorrow."

"Where did you hear that?

"I was down at the office and Marna was talking about changing the schedule to cover their shifts."

Stephanie had expected that something like this might happen. In a way she had hoped that it would. She thought that Shelly could do better for herself. Not that Jim was a bad guy, it was just that Kelly was shaping her life to fit his, giving up on the idea of children and to Stephanie that was a serious mistake. The greatest joy in Stephanie's life was her son. She knew that someday Shelly would come to regret not having a family.

"It doesn't surprise me, they argue all the time. Jim has not been around much and has left Shelly to fend for herself. I wonder if she's going back to live with her parents." Stephanie said.

"I don't know. I haven't talked to either of them much lately. "

"I tell you living in a campground is a lot like living in a fishbowl. You really get an up close look at the lives of your neighbors."

" Its funny when you think about our little corner of the universe and the people we share it with." Jason began.

"What do you mean?" Stephanie responded.

"Its hard to pretend when you live in such close quarter."

"Pretend?"

"When you live as close together was we have over the last few months, you can see how things really are. Not what someone wants you to see." Jason continued. "Shelly and Jim were destine to fail. They could pretend they were getting along, but living this close."

"Shelly reminds me of myself when I was young. My husband was older and I looked to him for his experience. I thought that I was in love with him and that he loved me back. I didn't look at the differences. The simple difference that I wanted children and he didn't."

"You also see the good stuff. The couples who made good marriages and are happy. It makes me sad in a way. I have been trying to have a family my entire life and failed. To see the success in Dale and Joyce or Mike and Hazel reminds me of never having what they have now."

"At least you understood and tried to make it happen for yourself. I just lived in my misery. I never had the courage to demand a change or take another path. I just accepted my fate."

"I didn't get it soon enough. I am afraid that I will never find love again. It's just not in the cards for me." Jason said. "Now, I just concentrate on being a good friend to the people in my life. I try to remember that connection is what is important."

"The connections in my life are very conditional." Stephanie said.

'Conditional?"

"I know all these people or should I say they know me. I can't go anywhere in my home town without people coming up and talking to me. Its always about their pets. I have this knowledge and it seems they want to know me because I am a Vet, not because of the person that I am. Its all superficial, I have very few close friends."

"A lot of what I did in my life was because I wanted to belong. Or the other way of saying it was that I was afraid of being disconnected. So I followed a sports team that everyone else liked. And it went on. It is very important to feel connected. To be a member of a tribe." Jason said.

"The people I know have no idea of who I was as a person. It feels like they are nice to me because they want something from me and not because of who I was as a person."

"Did they know the real you. Did anyone know you were unhappy?" Jason asked.

"No, I kept of the image of a happy marriage. I never talked to anyone about how I really felt. Not even my partners."

"So no one knew the real you. Why not?"

"I wanted them to like me. I guess that I didn't want anyone to know that I was failing in my marriage. I wanted to be seen as successful and happy."

"Why"

"I guess I would have been ashamed if they found out. Ashamed that I failed to make it work. And I didn't want them talking about me. Its a small town and everyone is alway in everybody else's business."

"How'd that work out for you?"

"Yeah."

CHAPTER FORTY-FOUR

The Dance

They were on one of their many trips to Cody for supplies. It had become their customer to grab a bite to eat when they were in Cody. Their normal routine put them in town around lunch and they had tried all the local lunch spots. On this trip, they had started later than usual and where in Cody in the early evening. Stephanie had wonder about the place near the west end of town called Cassie's Supper club. She suggested that they try this spot and Jason agreed.

Cassie's was a local favorite night spot. The exterior was rough sawn lumber and constructed in the board and batten style. A front porch with plank floors and picnic tables greeted you as you approached the entrance. Once in side you find yourself in a cross between an old west saloon, an art gallery, a museum and a dance hall. There isn't a spot on the wall that is filled with something Wyoming. They should charge admission just to view the interesting and varied history that is displayed through the building.

Stephanie and Jason entered and were lead to a table. They talked and laughed and ate their dinner. Jason attention turned towards the dance floor and he watched as the couples made their way around the floor. He turned back towards Stephanie. "They have a dance floor here." Jason began with a smile.

"I have never been dancing in my life" Stephanie replied.

"Why not? It against your religion"

"No, just busy with other things. Working, going to school, running a business, All that, never really had much time for dancing."

" I didn't dance much when I was young. I got into it after my first divorce. Sort of had to in order to met people. I found I liked it and began dancing regularly. Eventually got into country dancing. I liked it because you got to hold the girl.

Stephanie look around at the dance floor and notice there were a few couples slow dancing to the country music. "So you know how to dance like that? She asked.

Yes, they are doing the two step. It's easy to learn.

I can't dance, two left feet. Stephanie replied.

"Everyone can dance. All you have to do is rock back and forth to the music. The two step is a little more complicated, but not much."

"I don't know, I don't want to look stupid."

"You need to trust me, you will not look stupid. All you have to do is follow my lead and you'll do just fine."

Stephanie hesitated, not sure she could go out on the floor. This was out of her comfort zone. She never had time for dancing.

"Com' on, lets give it a whirl. You're thousands of miles from anyone who knows you and you will probably never see anyone in here again. "

Reluctantly Stephanie rose to go to the dance floor. As they walked from their table, Jason took her hand and led her to the floor. Stephanie knew enough to get into the stance right. She took Jason's left hand and place her other hand on his right shoulder. They were standing, facing at each other and Stephanie started to rock back and forth. Jason followed her lead and matched her rocking. She smiled and looked around the room to see if anyone was watching them. Everyone was engaged in their own lives and not paying attention to anything but themselves. Stephanie began to relax. Jason rocked back and forth with

Stephanie, not turning or moving about the floor. Jason tried to move Stephanie backwards by gently easing her in that direction. Stephanie lost her concentration and stumbled for a second.

"Stephanie." Jason began smiling. Dancing is one of the last places where the man is supposed to be in control. The guy is supposed to lead, the gal is supposed to follow. It works better that way."

Stephanie did not respond. She was too busy concentrating on her rocking and keeping to the beat of the music.

"You're thinking too much. You have to get out of your head. Dancing is more a feeling, more instinctual. You can think about it, but it becomes unnatural. You need to get out of your head and stop thinking about dancing."

"How do I do that?" Stephanie asked.

"You have to let go. Surrender."

"What do you mean?" Stephanie asked.

"Slow dancing is two people joining together to move in unison around the dance floor. It works best when one person decides where to go and what to do. You have to let go of control and follow the signals that my body gives you. You listen with your body, feeling my movements and not fighting them, but submitting and allowing yourself to be guided."

Stephanie did not respond. It was contrary to her nature to let someone else be in control, to submit to someone, anyone.

"If it is done right, then the dancers merge and become one, flowing effortlessly around the dance floor."

"I don't know. I'll give it a try. What do I do?"

"Just relax, stop thinking and start feeling. Listen to my hands. Feel the pressure when I gently push back on your hand. Or if I press on your back with my other hand. That's where we will start. Remember feel, not think."

Stephanie concentrate, focusing on not thinking. She felt Jason's hand in hers and on her back. Jason eased his hand forward and they started a slow turn to her right. Then he pressed against her back and withdrew his left hand and they began a slow turn in the opposite direction. They began to move around the dance floor, not just rocking from side to side. In no time at all they were turning and moving around the floor with ease.

"You're doing wonderful." Jason said. "Are you ready to try a little more?

"I don't know. I think we are doing great."

"Okay this will be fun. Again, you have to surrender to your partner and let him lead you. This time I want you to listen to my shoulders and my hips. Okay?"

"I'll try"

Jason pulled Stephanie closer to his body. They had be a full six inches apart. Now they were closer, almost touching. Stephanie's left arm was resting on Jason's and he held her left hand at a right angle to their bodies. Slowly Jason began turning his torso as they moved around the floor. This drew Stephanie closer to his body, touching at times. The spins and turns became faster and they drew closer together. Finally they were locked into an embrace, dancing and spinning around the floor. Stephanie could feel his body move. His chest would turn, and she would pivot around his hips as they spun and whirled around the dance floor.

The music continued as one song blended into another and they kept dancing, until the tempo slowed. The songs had been fast and she had to hold on to Jason as they danced. This was a slow song. It felt different to her, more personal, more intimate. As the song began, Jason continued holding her close, moving his left hand closer to their bodies, tucking it under his chin, causing her forearm to rest against his chest. She felt excited and safe at the same time. She relaxed and leaned into him pressing her body against his, resting her head on his chest. She was enveloped in his arms, mirroring his movements, swaying back and forth as his body moved, matching every turn and step. She felt the warmth of his body against hers, felt his breathing, listening to his heart beat. Jason took a deep breath, exhaling in a long slow moment.

Jason had given himself to the music, following the rhythm around the dance floor as if carried by the current through the rapids of a gently flowing river. He was not thinking, just responding, letting the music direct his movements. Stephanie had followed his every turn, following every clue his body gave as they moved around the floor. With his deep breath he was giving another clue, one he did not want to give, his breath was betraying him, revealing his attraction to Stephanie. Jason reacted fearing that Stephanie would understand, would know his feelings. He straightened his body and gently created space between them. Stephanie looked up at Jason and their eyes met and in that meeting no words were necessary, she knew. He pulled her close and she renewed her embrace, and for a moment holding him just a little tighter, telling him that she understood, that it was okay.

The song ended and they returned to their table. It was time to head back to the campground. They pointed the truck west and headed out of Cody. It was a moonless night and the darkness enveloped them as they drove. The headlights cut through the darkness, revealing their way through the void. Jason and Stephanie sat in silence as they road up the mountain.

CHAPTER FORTY-FIVE

Lewis Lake Hike

Jason knocked on Stephanie's door and waited for her response. Stephanie opened the door and invited him in. They were going on another hike today, they just needed to decide where to go. Stephanie had the Guide to Yellowstone open on the table.

"We can go along Lewis Lake following a cause way to Shoshone Lake." Stephanie suggested. "It's going to be a glorious day."

In the southwestern section of Yellowstone Park is a back country lake called Shoshone Lake. It is the largest back country lake in the lower forty-eight states. Back country is another way of saying visitors can't drive in their car anywhere close to the Lake. Two routes lead to the Lake, a trail or the lake is accessible by canoe or kayak. Lewis Lake is just to the southeast of Shoshone. Lewis Lake is accessible by car and is the launch point to reach Shoshone Lake by water. Connecting the two lakes is a causeway where water flows from Shoshone Lake down to Lewis Lake.

An eleven mile loop trail takes hikers along the edge of Lewis Lake to the causeway. From there, the trail follows the causeway to the shores of Shoshone Lake. Following the loop, the trail returns to the trail head through meadows and lodge pole pine forests. The trail is not very steep, just long. Jason knew that Stephanie wanted to go on this hike. When they had first started hiking together, they had begun the De Lacy trail which lead down to Shoshone Lake. They had to abandon the hike and went to the Lone Star Geyser instead.

"The walk was relatively flat and follows water the entire trip out." Jason replied.

Jason remembered that Stephanie was angry when he insisted on canceling the De Lacy hike. He did not want to go through that again. Jason had studied the trail guide too. He knew how long the trail was and it did not have a climb in elevation.

"Good, it's agreed. We will hike into Shoshone Lake." Stephanie said and Jason agreed.

The drive down to the trail head took them along the west side of Lake Yellowstone. It was early in the day and traffic was light. At the West Thumb area they turned left to head in the direction of the southern entrance to the park and in about ten miles the road meets the eastern shore of Lewis Lake and the parking lot for the trail head.

The lake was not visible from the trail head. The path headed off into an area that had been burned in one of Yellowstone's many fires. Pine trees had sprung up and reclaimed the area. The trees were thick and it was hard to see more than a few feet off the trail. The forest had not had the time to thin itself. With time, one tree will grow a little faster than the trees around it and claim more of the suns energy. Eventually the surrounding trees will die off, thinning out the forest. Stephanie and Jason broke out of the forest to the shores of Lewis Lake. The edge of the forest was set back two hundred yards from the water. The distance was covered with knee high grass growing in swamp or marsh like soil. The lake opened up and they could see across the lake all the way down to the Grand Tetons. The sun was shining with scattered clouds. The Grand Tetons were framed on the top by the blue sky and in front by the blue of Lewis Lake. It was a still day and the water was calm and flat. Painted on the water was a ghost image of the Tetons standing proud in the distance.

Stephanie and Jason found a fallen tree and sat for a moment, mesmerized by the view. They talked about nothing as they soaked in the scenery. After a spell, they returned to the trail and continued their hike. From the trail head, it was six miles to Shoshone Lake. They soon came to the causeway between the lakes. As they followed the causeway, they would occasionally see someone in a canoe or kayak making their way back from camping on the shores of Shoshone Lake. It was easy to imagine back to the days when travel by canoe was commonplace in this country. The quiet of the journey was only interrupted by the swirl of water around the paddle as it propels the canoe forward. Stephanie and Jason sat for a long time on the edge of a cliff that overlooked the waterway. They listened to the wind and felt its embrace as it would flow down the small valley between the two lakes.

Stephanie began to talk about her family as they walked. Stephanie was remembering her childhood. When she talked about her mother she glowed.

"My mother was a wonderful woman. She was kind and caring and the glue that held the family together." Stephanie said. "She insisted that we get together to celebrate the holidays, birthdays and other special occasions. After my mom passed, we stopped getting together."

They stopped along the way and sat by the water to eat their lunch. At the water's edge the shore was pebbles and rocks with sand. The pebbles and rocks were just a buffer between the water and a sea of grass that grew up between the lake and the wooded shores. The lake was a brilliant blue that was interrupted by the gray of the pebbles and the brown grass. The gray and brown were transformed by the vibrant green of the lodge pole pines and returned full circle to the blue of the Wyoming sky.

It was early afternoon and the wind was coming up. The color of the water darkened as the wind made the lake choppy. All the remote campsites dotted around the lake were empty. It was just Stephanie and Jason, in the vastness of the moment. Stephanie turned to Jason and watched him as he sat focused off over the water. Jason was here by himself. He had given her advice that made her think and gave her a new perspective on her life.

"How come you're not with someone?" Stephanie asked.

"It's a long story." Jason replied.

"It's a long walk back." Stephanie said.

"Somewhere, sometime, somehow, I came to believe that connections are not necessarily permanent. By connections I include lovers and friendships." Jason said

"Why do you say that?" Stephanie asked.

"That's been my experience. People who are my friends today will most probably not be my friends in five years. People just come in and out of my life. The people that I saw all the time five years ago, I do not see now."

Stephanie did not have the same life experience. She grew up in a small town and lived there her entire life. She had been married forever and knew just about everyone. Friendships were not fleeting to her. She knew people and they knew her, but did she have a connection with them or were they just characters that populated her life.

"How did you come to that conclusion?" Stephanie asked.

"When I was young I strove to be self-reliant. I used to think that the genesis for my desires for self-reliance was of my own making. In retrospect, it was more of a reaction to the uncertainty of the world I lived in. Truly, there was no one around that was there for me from a very young age."

Stephanie did not respond. She was thinking about her own life and how she could not rely on anyone either from a very early age. She was self-reliant. Jason continued.

"Needing someone, was something I decided was not for me."

"What do you mean?" Stephanie asked.

"I thought I could get along just fine on my own. I did not understand that connecting with other people is why we are here. It is in the connection with other people where we find purpose and meaning in our lives." Jason said.

181

Jason had not understood that the dysfunctions of his early life had played a role in his ability to connect with people. He did not feel good enough or deserving enough to be liked or to belong with other people. He fooled himself into believing he valued self-reliance and that striving for self-reliance was worthy of his effort. It was a defense to his fear of trying to connect with other people, especially someone special.

Later in life Jason came to a different understanding. Self-reliance was just a cover story. He began to understand what he was feeling was something different. He began to call this by another name, shame. He realized he was not letting people get to know him because of certain secrets he wanted to keep. These secrets were about his early childhood and his family.

"I was ashamed of some of my early life experiences. It took me some amount of time to understand how this shame was really the cause of my inability to connect with people and drove my reactions within the relationships that I did have, my shame was preventing me from connecting to other people in a healthy way." Jason said.

"How did you fix that?" Stephanie asked. "You don't seem like that person now."

"There was a time in my life when all I read was self-help. I'm alright, you're alright, and all that stuff. This is where it really hit home that my feelings of shame were centered on the fear of not being accepted. I was not worthy of friendship or I believed that there is something about me that if other people saw or knew, I would not be worthy of being their friend."

"That's sad. How'd you get passed that?" Stephanie asked.

"I worked on it a lot. I used to say that I was blessed with self-awareness but cursed with an inability to do anything with the knowledge. I just kept working at it, trying to understand why my relationships were not working." Jason said.

"What did you figure out?

"I don't know if I figured it out or just stumbled on a different way. I took myself out of the game. I stopped worrying about whether other people liked me or not. I just became myself and did not pretend to be someone else I believed I needed to be to have friends."

"I hear that all the time. I don't know what that means, be yourself." Stephanie said.

"For me it was a willingness not to be liked. I never really cared for sports, so I stopped pretending that I was interested. I wasted a lot of time watching football just to be liked. I liked eating at Denny's, so that's where I went, not P. F. Chang's or whatever was the restaurant of the week. I just did what made me happy." Jason said.

"How was that being yourself?" Stephanie asked.

I'm comfortable in blue jeans and tennis shoes. I could wear slacks with loafers, but I was more comfortable in jeans. So that's what I wore. I stopped worrying about what other people wore. This led to other things. My daughter got a little dog when she was young. He was a Pomeranian. That dog was the best dog we ever had, but I would not walk the dog around the block. I was afraid people might think I was gay or something."

Jason looked over at Stephanie and he could see that she didn't really get it.

"I decided to like the person that I was and not try to be someone else. I didn't care if someone else saw me in my fuzzy slippers. I was not perfect and I wasn't going to pretend that I was. I let down my guard with the people that I cared about. Remember when you first started dating and who said "I love you" first was an issue? Telling someone how you feel without any guarantee that they felt the same was scary. I told people how I felt without preconditions." Jason said.

"I care what other people think of me. I want to be liked." Stephanie said.

"I care what other people think too." Jason began. "I want people to like me too. The genuine person that I am, not a pretend person. If someone likes me for who I really am, that's a friend for life." Jason said.

Stephanie had to take some time to process this. She had spent her entire life cultivating an image. She had driven the right car, wore the right kind of clothes, and lived in the right part of town to create this image. She worried about what people would think. She had stayed in her marriage for years after the love had left. She kept up the image of a successful professional with a happy home life.

"All that doesn't really explain why there is no special someone in your life." Stephanie said.

"You're right. While I was coming to these conclusions, I was not interested in trying to connect with that special someone. I needed to understand it all first. It took some time and after I started to figure it out, I didn't feel the need to have a partner to make me whole. I was okay alone. If someone came along, that would be okay. But if I was alone, that would be okay too. As it worked out, no one came along." Jason answered.

"I don't want to live my life alone." Stephanie said.

"You are an attractive, smart and caring woman. You would have to beat the guys away with a stick." Jason replied.

Stephanie laughed and dismissed Jason's complement.

"I'm not just saying that. I know what I am talking about. I hope that I am not crossing a line here, but if I ran into you somewhere in the universe as a single woman, I would definitely be interested."

Stephanie looked over at Jason with a smile on her face. She paused for a moment and did not respond. She was gathering the courage to ask, afraid of the answer at the same time.

"You feel attracted to me?" She asked.

"I definitely feel that there is chemistry between us." Jason said without hesitation.

A flash of panic went through Jason. He immediately regretted blurting out that he felt chemistry for Stephanie. But there it was, out in the open. Jason paused for a minute, took a deep breath and decided that he had put one foot in the ring. He was going all in.

"Do you feel any chemistry for me?" Jason asked.

"Yes" came without hesitation.

The cards were on the table, there was chemistry between them. Stephanie and Jason sat in silence for a while.

Jason broke the silence. "We should be heading back, its a long walk."

They gathered up their gear and turned toward the trail back to the parking lot. The walk back was away from the water into gently rolling hills. The area had been burned by the firestorms of 1988. The new growth was thick and they could only see a short distance off the trail. They talked as they walked making as much noise as they could to alert any bears that they were coming down the trail. Eventually the trail met up with an abandoned road and it was another two miles of easy walking back to the parking lot.

CHAPTER FORTY-SIX

The End Nears

The season was coming to an end. There were more days behind them now that there were remaining. Everyone was counting down the days and talking about what they were going to do when they left Yellowstone. Stephanie had not planned that far ahead. She had focused on the change in her routine. Leaving her clinic and her home town where mixed in with her mission, her quest, to discover the roots of her unhappiness. Now she was faced with another decision.

A day like this does not happen often. Most days are just like any other. On occasion, there are days that change the rest of your life. Sometimes you recognize the change when it happens, sometimes you only understand after the fact. This day would change Stephanie's life forever and she knew it. She had come to the conclusion that her marriage had been over for years and no one bothered to tell her. She was not in love with her husband and he probably only saw her as the major source of funds for his retirement plan.

She smiled as she pictured Jason and the remembered the times that they had spent together. She had not felt attracted to anyone in as long as she could remember. Here in this far away place, away from the world, she had met Jason. He had a strength of resolve that she had never seen before. His kindness was apparent to anyone who bothered to look. He wasn't afraid to open himself up and allow a look inside, revealing his honest feelings. Stephanie had no experience with honest vulnerability. She was always guarded, always dealing with walls and constructed appearances. She had truly never met anyone like Jason and this was scary for her. Scary and exciting, igniting feeling and emotions that she had not experienced since she was a young girl. Before she married and settled for a life without passion, without love.

Stephanie imagined a her life different, a life with Jason. She daydreamed about what it may have been like if they had met when she was young. She imagined falling in love with Jason, having his children, and the adventures the would have shared together. What it would be like to be love by a man who could and wanted to make her feel their time together was something to be cherished.

A feeling of regret rose up inside her. She had wasted her life, waiting for something that was impossible. Everyday hoping that this would be the day her marriage would change and he would look at her, see her, feel her, love her. At long last, she realized that this was never to be, no matter how much she wanted a different result, she had to make a change. Tears welled up in her eyes that turned to drops running down her cheeks. She cried softly, sad at the understanding that she had to start a new life. That she could never go back, never return to the Tennessee that she had known all her life, never go back to the way things were.

CHAPTER FORTY-SEVEN

Avalanche Peak

Stephanie went into the bedroom and opened the drawer by her bed. She took out the black bag, put it in her backpack and headed out for her solo hike to Avalanche Peak. There were no hiking partners for her today, Jason had to work and no one else was available. She decided to take the opportunity to go on this challenging hike.

As she drove along the lake heading east towards the Sylvan pass, she reflected on the events and circumstances that led her to Yellowstone. She thought about her marriage, her career, and her husband. Since coming to Yellowstone, she had gained clarity. She saw her life in Tennessee for the illusion that it was. She was pretending she was happy, pretending she was living a fulfilling life with a successful marriage and career. She did not want to pretend anymore.

She pulled her car into the parking lot at the trailhead. The walk up the trail was strenuous, and she had to make frequent stops along the way to catch her breath. All the while she was reviewing, thinking about the last few months, her time in Yellowstone. Thinking about what she now appreciated, what she now valued, what she now wanted. She followed a Creek for a while eventually having to cross it. She came to the site of an old burn, where charred trees were surrounding by flowered meadows. After crossing through a large bowl like structure she encountered rocky barren terrain. Eventually she made it up to the top of Avalanche Peak.

From the peak she had a 360° view in every direction. The peak was over 10,000 feet in elevation. She was able to see to the East out of the Park and to the all the vast openness that laid towards Cody. She found herself an outcropping and set for a while thinking about her life, her future. She took her backpack off and took the black bag out of the pack. She opened the bag and look at the vile of drugs and the needle. She remembered the thousands of pets whose life she had ended with this drug. She consoled herself with the thought that the pets she had euthanized had lived their lives in a loving home and had wonderful lives. That ending their lives was the last expression of love and caring that the owner showed for their pet.

She took the vile of drugs out of her bag and held it in her hand looking at it. She reached into her coat pocket and pulled out her pocketknife. She opened the blade and inserted it in the rubber membrane that sealed the vile of drugs. She slowly turned boring a hole through the membrane. She upended the bottle and watched the drugs run down splashing on the rocks below.

CHAPTER FORTY-EIGHT

Kiss on the bank

Stephanie and Jason were traveling up the west side of the Grand Loop road. They were spending some time revisiting the Old Faithful area. The day had begun with a walk around the board walk at Old Faithful. They had been there before and witnessed the eruption of Old Faithful Geyser but had declined to walk the boardwalk. Old Faithful is the most visited place in the park. In terms of hiking this was low hanging fruit. It was flat and easily accessible and it was crowded. Because of the crowds, they decided that they would wait until later in their stay at Yellowstone to explore this area. That time had come.

As they walked along the boardwalk they talked. Stephanie and Jason had put words to their attraction for each other. Jason had told her he was attracted to her and she had admitted the same for him. They had continued to spend all of their free time together, talking and sharing as they explored the park. The end of the season was approaching and soon it would be time to leave Yellowstone and start the next chapter in their lives. Jason had imagined more between them and he now wanted something more. He longed to reach out, hold her near and to feel her embrace as she held him.

Jason took every opportunity to make physical contact with Stephanie as they walked the boardwalk. These were casual fleeting touches, brushing up against her when trying to get a look at something while in a crowd or touching her shoulder to draw her attention.

They finished walking the Old Faithful Boardwalk and they started driving north on the Grand Loop Road. Yellowstone has a lot to offer visitors. Originally the park was designed to be toured by automobile. A tourist could literally drive up to a thermal feature and view it without ever getting out of their car. In some areas of the park this is still possible.

Just east of the road going north from Old Faithful there is an area that can be viewed from a vehicle. It is a loop off the main road. In this place the water seeps from what seems like every nook and cranny in the ground. The water appears to sheet across the landscape until it finds a capillary of a stream or brook to carry it off. The water is heated and ladened with minerals that color the ground in various shades and hues. The ground in the area is hot from heat rising from far below the surface. Earlier in the season, the asphalt roads began to melt and had to be closed to traffic. The area cooled down and eventually traffic was allowed back into the area. It's hard to describe the feelings one gets when in a place like this. There must have been a time when much more of the world was like this. When the world was young and life was just getting started. When the warm mineral rich water fed the fledging life forms that struggled to survive around the fringes of such a hostile place.

Being in such a place grounds a person, centers them and brings into perspective the value or importance we place on things and events in daily life. Jason was sitting in the passenger seat of a truck driven by a truly rare and amazing lady. She had touched a part of him that he had imagined was long dead. Jason had hidden his heart from even the possibility that there was a special someone in the world to find. And here in the remote reaches of Yellowstone his granite facade had been cracked. His possibilities had been redefined. Here was someone who could make him feel like a teenager in love.

All this was true, but the truth of it did not matter. Stephanie was married. Jason had always believed that he never wanted to be the cause of the breakup of a marriage. He had his ethos, his rules for living his life. Jason's feelings for Stephanie violated his rules. Feelings were only feelings, the question was would he act upon them. If Stephanie reached out for him, would he respond or would he pull away and end any chance that their lives would join. Would Jason refuse any chance for lasting love and happiness?

Jason looked over at Stephanie as they turned back onto the main road. Stephanie had a wistful distant look about her.

"What are you thinking about?" He began.

Stephanie smiled and turned to look at him. She didn't respond immediately but returned her gaze to the road ahead. A moment passed and she looked back over at Jason and smiled. "I was thinking about going home to Tennessee. I really don't want to go back. I was so unhappy there and I have lived that life for as long as I can. Now, I want to live the life that I want to live. I want to travel and see the country. I want to live the life I want to live and not the one they expect me to live."

"I understand a little about that." Jason replied. They drove on, returned to the main road and headed north towards Madison. They came to a left turn off the main road.

"You ever been down this Road?" Jason asked.

"Nope" Stephanie replied.

"Well let's see where it goes, what do you say? He said

"Sounds good to me." Replied Stephanie.

They turned left and the road started following the Firehole River. They drove for about a mile and the road ended in a parking lot. It was Fountain Flat Drive that followed the Firehole River away from the main road. The parking lot was almost empty and Stephanie pulled into a spot. One of the places that was on their list to visit on this trip was a swimming hole on the Firehole River. They had heard about the swimming hole on the first tour of the park. They had learned that the Firehole River got twenty-five percent of its water from thermal features. Most of the rivers and streams in Yellowstone are too cold to swim in. The heated water from thermal features made the Firehole River about the only place a person could swim without turning into a Popsicle.

"Let's walk down to the river" she said.

"Sounds good, let's go."

They got out of the truck and without saying much walked the short distance to the banks of the River. Stephanie found a place to sit and Jason followed her lead. A gentle slope of two or three feet led down to the water's edge. The water moved by slow and easy. The occasional floating object was only way to tell the water was moving.

They were just below Madison Junction. This area runs from the Old Faithful area north to the Madison area and is filled with fields of thermal features. It includes the upper and lower geyser basins. The Firehole River meanders through the valley. The place that they had just been through was other worldly. The contrast in landscapes could not have been more striking. There was the lone buffalo in the distance grazing and oblivious to everything else around him. As they sat on the bank, they saw several ducks drifting just upstream of them on the river. The ducks would find eddies in the current and floated in a small group. At some undetectable clue, all the duck would go bottoms up, sticking their heads under water with their tails sticking straight up in the air. Shortly thereafter they would start popping up, one after another until that all returned upright again. On occasion they would get caught in the current and float passed them down the river. By some unseen means of propulsion they would return to their starting spots and the routine would begin again. As they sat watching the world turn, the occasional trout would fling himself out of the water and plop back in again. They could see small white insects hovering just above the water and they assumed that the trout were interested in eating these white bugs. They followed a specific bug to see if a trout jumped at it,

193

but were never able to confirm that the white bugs were indeed the targets of the trout.

They sat by the stream and watched the world turn. Off in the distance were the mountains that framed the valley where they sat. The mountains were miles away and proceeded by a vast open plain. It was hard to judge distance in Yellowstone. Jason imagined crossing the flat land and coming to the base of the mountains. He asked himself how long that would take. After crossing that space he would be at the base of mountains that would be even more daunting. He could not imagine the effort that it would take to cross that barrier. Jason was contemplating crossing a barrier. He had feelings for Stephanie. They had discussed this and he had told her that he felt there was chemistry between them. They were in this place together, sitting on the side of a river soaking in the sheer beauty that is Yellowstone. Stephanie, beholding the expanse to the mountains beyond, began:

"Yellowstone really gives you a different prospective. You can't help but see the problems of your daily life in different terms. It changes what you think is important and the value that you place on the things in your life. It's like instead of seeing only your little corner of the world, for the first time I get a glimpse of how vast the world is and just how little a part of it my own life is."

"It certainly does. But I wouldn't sell yourself short. If you take the whole universe, there are billions and billions of stars out there. In the entire universe there is only one Stephanie. You are indeed amazingly unique." Jason replied.

"I know, but when you sit out here, it puts your life in perspective. How important are my flower beds and do they have to be completely weed free? I have been unhappy for a very long time. I have been reluctant to make any changes and have just endured in an unhappy life. Hoping that things would change and my life would get better. I just don't want to be alone. I am afraid that if I change things that I will live the rest of my life alone."

Jason sat there thinking to himself, wondering about his future. Wondering if this moment would ever present itself again. He was sitting on the bank of a river in an incredible environment with Stephanie just inches away from him. They had never been closer. They had shared their feelings, their hopes and dreams for the future. Stephanie was worried about her future. She had awakened feeling in him that he had given up as lost forever. Could he cross the divide? Could he take the risk and bare his soul to another. Open himself up to the possibility of the heartache and desperation that comes from love lost or forgotten.

Stephanie started talking about the unfilled wants in her life. She had worked hard and wanted the rewards of her efforts. She wanted to love life again, a love that had been stolen by years of a bad marriage. She wanted to explore the world and experience the awe and wonder of nature in all its many expressions. All Jason could think about was that he wanted to kiss her. He knew that there was a possibility that he would create an awkwardness between them that might turn bad. It might be too soon. It might be too late. It might not be right.

Jason waited for the right moment, a quite spot to begin. Stephanie was talking about what she had always wanted. So he began.

"I have always wanted to be in a beautiful spot along an easy flowing river, sitting on its banks with someone special."

Stephanie's focus was still off in the distance. Stephanie's focus came back to the river bank and a slight smile came across her face.

"I have always wanted to kiss a girl on the bank of a river." He continued.

Stephanie's smile widened and she turned her head slightly in his direction. He leaned slightly towards her and she slowly turned into his path. They moved closer to each other and drew into a soft gentle embrace. They paused, her lips touching his, each of them holding their breath. It was a mere moment that

195

Jason wanted to remember always. He leaned back and Stephanie turned back to the river. They sat in silence as the ducks bobbed in the river, exploring the unseen territory beneath the surface of the water.

CHAPTER FORTY-NINE

Ranger Program and a walk in the dark

National parks often have ranger led programs and talks. Yellowstone was no different. Right across the highway from fishing Bridge RV Park was a visitor's center. Each visitor center had and amphitheater where every night a different ranger talk was presented. These ranger talks usually lasted for thirty minutes to one hour depending on the complexity of the issue covered. The talks included the local wildlife, the geological features of the park, and the parks history.

Jason and Stephanie's primary focus had been walking and hiking in the back country. Working at the RV park they often stayed in the office until eight or nine o'clock on their work shifts. This translated into little opportunity or desire to attend a ranger talk. It seemed that attending a ranger talk was becoming a more important priority to them as time went on. Although both Stephanie and Jason had been to ranger talks in the past, they had not been to one in Yellowstone. It seemed like at least one ranger talk had to be attended in order to claim that they fully experienced all that Yellowstone had to offer.

It was decided, they would go to a ranger talk. They chose one that featured the history of the early explorers of the Yellowstone region and where the ranger talk was at the Fishing Bridge Visitor Center. These talks were almost always after dark and were accompanied by a slide presentation narrated by a park ranger.

Stephanie and Jason made their way across the road and found the amphitheater. They took up seats on one of the long parklike benches. Stephanie sat to Jason's right and waited for the ranger talk to begin. Stephanie sat close to Jason, closer than a casual friend would sit. Her leg brushed up against his and he could feel the fabric of her coat rubbing against his. They listened attentively to the ranger as he recounted the early history of the exploration of the Yellowstone area.

The program came to a conclusion and it was time to walk back to the RV park. It was a moonless night and there wasn't much in the way of light around the Fishing Bridge area. Away from any structure, a flashlight was required to be able to see the way. It was as dark as dark could be. Stephanie and Jason had walked all over the area and had intimate knowledge of Fishing Bridge and the Visitor's Center. They decided to take a shortcut back to the RV park. Their path took them across the road and behind the general store. Behind the store there was a ball field and dirt roads that crisscrossed the area. They had walked it many times and recognized the features as they walked towards the campground. The voices of the visitors around the store began to fade away as they approached the center of the ball field. Jason was shining his light ahead to lead them through the field.

"Hold up a sec." Jason said.
"What's up?" Stephanie asked.

Jason turned off the light and stood for a second in the darkness that enveloped them. He was standing next to Stephanie, shoulder to shoulder. He turned towards her and found the back of her shoulder with his hand. At the same time Stephanie turned her body to meet his. Jason's hand slipped down her shoulder to the small of her back as he pulled her closer. She raised her right hand placing it on his chest as she drew near. Jason's left hand cradled the back of her arm and slid across her back closing their embrace. They held tight to each other in the darkness of the

198

field. Away from the world, away from the prying eye of the campground. It was just the two of them and the world did not matter. They had crossed a divide and reached out for the embrace that they had both wished for, waited for, longed for. They held each other for just a moment. They did not dare risk a longer embrace. But it was enough for now.

CHAPTER FIFTY
Trailer

By the time they reached the campground it was close to ten o'clock. It was quiet as they walked down the loop toward the employee section of the park. The office had been closed for almost an hour. All the other employees were tucked in for the evening. Stephanie and Jason walked silently as they approached her trailer. Stephanie leaned into Jason and whispered "Come in for a minute."

Stephanie unlocked the door and they quickly stepped inside the trailer. Stephanie flipped a switch and a small accent light broke the darkness. Stephanie surveyed the trailer and moved to shut a curtain behind the dinette. Jason stood next to the door and waited for Stephanie to finish.

Stephanie turned and looked at Jason, pausing as she finished sealing out the rest of the world. She remained silent as she crossed the space between them. Jason turned towards her as she approached. He took a step in her direction and Stephanie moved closer. She stopped, standing in front of Jason, lost in his eyes. She took a breath and held it in. Jason brought his hand up and cupped the back of Stephanie's left elbow. In unison Stephanie closed the distance between them. Her right hand came up to his chest as she met his embrace. Her lips were warm and soft as he gently pressed himself into her. He felt the warmth of her body against his. Jason wrapped his arms around her, pulling her in.

Stephanie folded into the embrace. Their bodies gently turning and swaying as they came together.

Without a word, Stephanie took Jason by the hand, turned and walked up the stairs towards the bedroom. There was a pause as they reached the bed. They stood looking into each other's eyes. Asking an unspoken question. Stephanie stepped closer to Jason, and softly kissed his lips.

CHAPTER FIFTY-ONE

The morning after

They woke up together in each other's arms. Jason was lying on his back and Stephanie was pressed up against his side with her head resting on his chest. They clung to each other, immersed in the moment, enveloped in the warmth of each other's bodies. The world was outside and that was where they wanted it to stay. For now, it was just the two of them. Nothing else mattered.

They clung to the moment as long as they could. Neither one of them wanting to lift the veil that kept reality at bay. Outside the world was unchanged, but for them, there was a new beginning. New possibilities.

"Good Morning" Jason said as he kissed Stephanie's forehead and tightened his embrace. Stephanie gently rubbed Jason's chest and kissed his cheek. "I don't want it to be morning." She said as she pressed her body into Jason's.

Jason turned towards Stephanie, pulling her up and kissed her on her lips. Stephanie mirrored his soft embrace as his lips gently turned in a circular motion, pressing in then drawing back. Stephanie's response to the rhythm of his kiss slowly moved into her body. Jason reached behind her, followed the contour of her spine up her back, tightening his embrace, pressing his chest into hers. She moaned as her body responded to Jason's touch. They merged together, body and soul, making love in the early morning light. Wishing it could last forever.

The days that followed flew by as the date the park closed grew closer. In public they acted as if nothing had changed. They were coworkers and hiking buddies. They stole away, finding private moments, embracing in the shadows, keeping up appearances.

CHAPTER FIFTY-TWO

confessions

Jason and Stephanie kept exploring the park. When they couldn't get away from the campground, they walked down the sewer road to the waste water treatment plant. They were halfway down the road to the plant when the conversation took a serious note.

"We need to talk." Stephanie began.

For Jason, those four words had never been a welcome opening remark. "We need to talk" was always the precursor to a problem.

"There is something I need to tell you." Stephanie began. "There is more to the story. The true story."

"What are you talking about" Jason asked relieved just a bit.

"You and I have shared a lot about our lives. I have talked to you about the fact that I am trying to understand why I am unhappy." Stephanie continued. "I haven't told you everything. There are things that I have not shared with anyone."

Jason listened with anticipation. He flashed back to the text message that he had seen on Stephanie's cell phone. He remember Stephanie's body language, how she was shut down, cowering in a way. He had wondered about the reason for such a response.

"There are things that I think you should know. Things that make my life more complicated. Things that I need to take care of before we can start a life together." Stephanie said. "The problem is that I can't deal with it all right now. I don't even want to think about it."

Jason was a little taken aback. He was still elated, seeing the world through rose colored glasses. Now he was getting a dose of maybe its not as good as he thought.

Jason was stunned by the conversation. Just a couple of months ago he was alone in the world with no possibility of a connection with a special someone. He was disappointed by this state of affairs, but he had resigned himself to the situation. He had met Stephanie and fell in love. It was not his plan, it had just happened. She had expressed feelings for him and they had joined together. Now that future was threatened.

"I need to go back and finish what I started." Stephanie said. "I think it is a bad idea to start something new before I finish things back home."

"There's no need to go back now." Jason protested. "We need more time together. We need to build a little on our foundation. More shared memories. We need a couple more months together."

Stephanie did not respond. Jason finally broke the silence.

"I'm afraid." Jason started. "I don't want to lose you. I'm afraid if you go back home, I'll never see you again."

Jason was worried on more than one level. They had found each other and fell in love. Stephanie had shared that her life was more complicated than he had imagined. What was she going back to. How could he just watch her walk away?

"I will find you. I will go home and end my marriage and then I will find you." Stephanie assured him.

"I'm begging you, don't do this now. Jason pleaded. "Give us a better chance. We can go to Utah and spend time in Moab or Bryce. We can explore the canyons and maybe get a job working in one of those parks for a while.

"I've thought a lot about this." Stephanie replied. "I love you and I really want to see where we can go together. I just can't start that until I take care of making the past be in the past."

Jason was devastated. There was nothing he could say. She's going back to her husband. Jason hadn't said "I love you" to a woman in years. Jason needed to find a way to get through these remaining days. How could he stay sane and not break down. He asked himself "Am I a mere dalliance to her?" He could not tell one way or the other. "It's all good." He told himself.

After returning from the hike, they went to her trailer for dinner. They talked while they prepared a meal, avoiding any mention of what was going to happen at the end of the season. They ate and talked some more. Then they downloaded the pictures from her camera and remembered the hikes they took as they viewed the photographs.

Finally they went to bed, falling asleep in each other's embrace.

CHAPTER FIFTY-THREE

The End of a Season

The season at Yellowstone was coming to an end. The RV park was closing on September 23rd and all of the employees had to be out of the park not later than September 25th. Jason knew this day was coming. He had begged and pleaded with Stephanie for another path, a different result. Jason wanted to extend their time together. Stephanie did not have to go back home. There was nothing there for her. She was going to get divorced, but that did not have to happen now. It could be in three months.

Stephanie had repeatedly said that she did not want to start anything until she had finished what she had already started. They had already started, but somehow that didn't count. Jason was going back to Nevada. He had lost his zeal to travel alone and needed to be in the company of friends and around familiar faces. The park slowly emptied out. It got down to just Stephanie and Jason.

Jason helped Stephanie hook up her trailer. She was ready to hit the road. Jason had started the bus. It took about twenty minutes for the bus to warm up. Then it would be time to leave.

There wasn't much to say. It had all been said in the days leading up to this moment. It was time to go. Jason walked over to Stephanie and took her in his arms. He hugged her tight, lingering in the embrace. He released his hold, pulling back and looking into Stephanie's eyes. He leaned forward and softly kissed her lips. Stephanie's eyes were full of tears as she returned Jason's embrace. Jason stepped back and turned to walk back to his bus. He did not say goodbye, he did not say a word. Stephanie turned and walked to her truck.

Jason got into the bus and sat in the driver's seat. He paused, allowing the moment to sink in. He put the bus in first gear and slowly let the clutch out. The bus inched forward and turned down the loop road towards the entrance to the park. Jason checked his mirrors and saw Stephanie following him out of the Campground. Jason and Stephanie both turned right at the main road. It was just over a mile to the T intersection on the other side of Fishing Bridge. Jason turned right to head through West Yellowstone and back down to Las Vegas. He watched his rear view mirror. Stephanie pulled to a stop and turned left, towards West Thumb, Jackson and then the east coast.

CHAPTER FIFTY-FOUR
Old Buffalo-bear

The old buffalo was grazing in the west end of Hayden Valley. Scattered about the landscape, off in the distance were the black dots of other lone male buffalo. He was lame and it pained him to move. One of his eyes was swollen near shut from a bite from the wolf he had recently gored. He walked slowly, his movements deliberate and guarded. Swinging his head right to left has he grazed the valley floor and slowly marched forward.

The old buffalo felt the impact of a thousand pounds on his back. It was a big male Grizzly. The bear had used an old creek bed to ease up on the buffalo. The bear waited until the buffalo was close, biding his time as the buffalo slowly walked into range. The bear's charge happened to be on the buffalo's bad side, the one with the swollen eye. The buffalo never saw him coming. The bear landed on the buffalo's back, his four inch claws reaching out and grabbing the buffalo on the opposite side of his back, digging into flesh. The bear bit down on the spinal cord and the buffalo arched his neck and attempted to pivot around in the direction of the bear. The bear held on and spun with the buffalo, staying out of reach of the horns, the only weapon the buffalo had. It was over in just a few moments. The buffalo fell and the bear spun around to be away from the kicking legs of the buffalo. The bear moved toward the head of the old buffalo and clamped down on the throat, cutting off the flow of blood to the brain. The buffalo slowly lost consciousness, drifted into a dreamlike state and died from lack of oxygen to the brain.

The bear would have a full stomach tonight. He would stand guard over his kill and chase away any other would be diners. The wolves would come back, but they were no match to a full grown grizzly guarding a fresh kill. They would check back later, after a couple of days and see if there was anything left by the bear. For now they moved off looking for a less dangerous way to find a meal.

CHAPTER FIFTY-FIVE

epilouge

The call came in at about seven in the evening when Jason was in his favorite restaurant in Las Vegas. He had returned to Vegas to recover from the shock over Stephanie's decision to return home.

Stephanie was in Tennessee. She had returned home and ran into an emotional firestorm. Her husband had changed to the point where she did not recognize him. For the entire time that she had known him, it was alway him against the world. He was unethical in his dealing with other people, taking whatever advantage when and where he could. This was an aspect of his character that Stephanie did not like. She was surprised when he started treating her in this manner. It became apparent that it was not going to be an amicable divorce.

"Hello" Jason said with anticipation in his voice.

"Hi there" Stephanie responded.

"Good to hear your voice." Jason began. "How are things."

"That's why I called.' Stephanie said. "Things are tougher than I thought they would be. The divorce is going to be messy.

"I'm sorry." Jason said.

"Its okay. I'll get through it. But I have changed my plans. I rented an apartment and I want you to come out and live with me." Stephanie said.

Jason was stunned, he had not expected this. He had steeled

himself for a couple of months at least and the possibility that they would never see each other again.

"Wow," is all that Jason could manage to get out.

"I miss you more than I can say, and it looks like I am going to be stuck here for a while. I want you to fly out and stay with me." Stephanie said.

They talked about the details and the arrangements were made. Jason put his bus in storage and he was on a plane heading to Chattanooga, heading to the Mountains of Tennessee.

Made in the USA
Columbia, SC
06 February 2023

11112133R00117